Ocean's Widow

DEMELZA CARLTON

ISBN-13: 978-1-925799-28-6
ISBN-10: 1-925799-28-X

DEDICATION

This book is for Mum, who always wants to see more historical fiction set in Western Australia, so I figured it was my turn. History even helped by breaking a bridge for me.

One

He died because you left him, my traitorous heart whispered.

I wouldn't ask again. We'd searched for wreckage for three weeks, before even the captain gave up hope and our coal stocks ran dangerously low. Every morning since the ship had arrived in port, I'd asked at the newsagent as I bought the daily newspaper. Always the same question.

"Any news of the *Trevessa*?"

Every day for a week, Mrs Capper shook her head sadly.

This morning, I didn't want to meet her pitying eyes and believe that William was lost.

I laid my paper on the counter and wondered where she was.

"Are you going to buy those comic books?" the elderly lady thundered. I heard a squeaky sound. "Then get out of my shop before I tan your hides!" Two small children bolted out the door, pursued by Mrs Capper, brandishing a rolled-up newspaper. Once the children were out of sight, she smiled for me. "Good morning, Maria. Just the morning paper?"

I nodded, placing two pennies on the counter.

She took my coins and tucked them into her till. "Aren't you going to ask?"

This time, I shook my head and tucked the folded paper under my arm, shuffling dejectedly out of her shop.

"The lifeboats reached land. The papers are full of it – the telegram reached London last night."

I lifted desperate eyes to her face. If she toyed with my heart, buoying my hopes only to dash them… I slapped my newspaper on the counter. "Show me," I begged.

The paper crackled as she turned the pages and dragged her finger down the columns until she reached a well-spaced headline that spanned two columns. "There. You can read it yourself."

So close. I stroked the page that could tell me William's fate – or it would, if I could only read the words. "No. I can't. Please…"

Now I saw her pity, but it didn't lance my heart the way it had yesterday. She shook out the page and squinted at the close print. "Nothing stirs the human mind more acutely or fires the imagination to greater heights than a thrilling story of heroism and endurance at sea…" She continued until she found the names of those who'd died before the lifeboat reached land. "What is your sweetheart's name, Maria?"

"McGregor. William McGregor." My voice surrounded his name like a caress, wishing the words were the wonderful man himself. The man who'd saved me, protected me, fought for me and loved me. Whose lifeboat had been separated from mine when the stormy swell tore us apart.

Her finger traced the letters as I held my breath. "Someone named Jacobali. What sort of strange foreign name is that?"

I remembered three dark-skinned men, grinning at me as they festooned the mess hall with red-painted toilet paper streamers for the chief officer's birthday party. That was the night before the ship sank. All three had been named Ali. I wondered which had been Jacob Ali. Now I'd never know. "Who else?" I managed to say, forcing back tears.

"A...Nagi. Another foreign name. Both firemen, it says. Coloured men, probably." She gave a sniff.

Firemen worked the boiler room. All the men who'd worked with the boilers were the same colour – black from coal dust, tinted red and orange in the firelight. I carefully noted her strange comment, intending to ask Aunt Merry about it when I reached home.

"Where are they?"

She peered at the paper. "Rodriguez Island, it says. Sounds foreign, too. Oh, wait…the paper says it's in the Indian Ocean, somewhere near the colony at Mauritius. That's almost as far away as India!"

The other side of the Indian Ocean – as far from me as the ocean could cast him. What were the chances he'd cross that vast distance to return to me?

"Your sweetheart's alive, girl! Why aren't you grinning from ear to ear?" Mrs Capper demanded.

I forced myself to smile. "I'll do that when I see him again. I am…relieved and happy." I hoped she didn't notice my hesitation as I fought to find the right words. Three weeks of intensive English lessons with Aunt Merry had helped, but my vocabulary was woefully limited – even with my memory. I'd begun to relive my experiences with William, a little each day and more when I lay in bed, avoiding sleep. Remembering every kiss, every caress and every word that I hadn't understood at the time, but was coming clear the more I learned.

He'd said he loved me and wanted no future without me. He'd wanted me to be his wife, but I hadn't understood what he was asking then and he'd known that, swearing he'd ask me later when I could answer. Never knowing that later might never come.

I maintained my smile as I bade her farewell, folded my newspaper under my arm, and headed home to tell Aunt Merry the good news.

William was alive. If only he didn't believe I was dead.

Two

I almost cried with relief as I trudged home. For the first time, I felt no irritation at my flapping bloomers or constricting bandeau, nor the long skirt that tangled around my legs with every step I took into the stiff southerly breeze. I didn't even notice the fresh, Antarctic temperature of the wind, I was so happy. I could love a man without killing him, for William lived.

"So the news is true and your man is among the living," Aunt Merry greeted me from the front veranda.

I nodded and opened the screen door to head inside in search of breakfast.

Merry's arm barred my way. "Now, we didn't spend all those weeks locked in a cabin to keep you hidden from the crew, practicing your English for you not to speak to me. Tell me, Maria."

I swallowed. "A lifeboat reached some islands on the far side of the Indian Ocean. Two men died, but the rest lived. Including William. I know no more than that, Aunt Merry. Perhaps if you read the newspaper, you can tell me more than I know."

She lifted her arm to permit me to pass, but she followed me inside. "I think you know more than you've told me, Maria. I need to know what happened to you if I'm to continue to help you and so will everyone else. All anyone knows is that you're my niece – and we both know that's not true."

I remained silent as I cut some bread and spread Aunt Merry's homemade mulberry jam in a thick, purple layer across the slightly stale slice. My teeth crunched through the crust and the tart sweetness hit my tongue. I'd never tasted anything this good.

Merry poked the coals in the wood stove and added some kindling. She shifted the kettle to the spot over the newly kindled flame before spooning fresh tea into her immaculate teapot. "We're almost out," she said softly. "Can you go to the Chinese grocer's this week to get some more? The way you drink tea, we'll be using a tin a week."

I nodded. She'd provided me with food, shelter, clothing and the ability to communicate in her language. The least I could do was run errands for her — and hope she would soon tell me how I could repay my debt to her. But not with my secrets. No, I couldn't tell this kind woman about my past.

She bustled about, brewing tea in silence. As she set our cups on the table, I realised the huge differences between us. Like her delicate china cup and saucer, Merry's impeccable appearance contrasted strongly with my tin mug and layers of ill-fitting clothes. As she poured milk into her cup, turning her dark brew into a creamy, opaque light tan, mine remained a translucent, murky brown. "You should try it with milk," she admonished, but I shook my head and lifted the cup to my lips. I could manage to drink it like this, but the milk seemed to intensify the muddy flavour that made me feel ill.

Merry enthroned herself at the head of the kitchen table. "This time, I think you know enough English to tell me the truth – and I'll know if you're lying. Let's start at the beginning. Where are you from?"

I gulped a mouthful of tea, letting the hot liquid burn its way down the inside of my chest. "From the islands of Cocos. Far to the north, near India."

She nodded slowly. "A colonial girl. That would explain your queer notions of clothing and your complete lack of English." She sipped her tea. "Who was your father?"

My father? This question swam perilously close to my secrets. "A cable-man at Cocos," I said finally. "Telegraph cable."

Another nod. "His name? Tell me his name and yours."

I shook my head. "My name is Maria. That is all."

"What about your mother?"

"She…lives. Will not see me. I am disgraced. She sent me away." I filled my mouth with tea before I could say any more.

Merry's eyes widened with surprise. "What did you do?"

I smiled faintly. "I loved a man. A fish-man. A good man, but he could not swim. There was a big storm and his boat threw him into the water. The boat sank and he died."

Her eyes held more tears than mine, though a tear for Giuseppe already trickled down my cheek. "A fisherman. You're a fisherman's widow?"

Widow. William had used this word to describe me, but I didn't know it. "I don't know the meaning of this word. Widow?"

"When…when your husband – the man you love – dies, then you are no longer his wife. You are a widow. A widow is a wife whose man has left her."

I nodded. "Fish-man…no, fisherman's widow. Yes."

She leaned across the table and captured my hand. Her fingers were smaller than mine and roughened from hard work, but her grip was surprisingly firm. "I'm sorry, Maria. To lose the man you love is a hard thing. How long ago did he die?"

"Two years," I said. It was longer than that – Giuseppe had drowned in a summer cyclone and we were in the middle of winter now – but the wound was still fresh. "He called me Maria Stella Maris – his lady of the sea, who would always save him. And I couldn't. I couldn't save him from the sea." My tears spilled over, as if my salt-water heart had burst, and I pressed my face to the table so she wouldn't see my weakness.

"It's all right. You couldn't save him. No one can fight the ocean."

A smile crept to my lips and laughter struggled to escape. I'd fought the ocean and lost, but still I fought. Each battle was a test, the ocean's trial of my strength, for one day, I would win. I pressed my forehead harder against the wood, hoping she didn't see my fierce grin.

"How did you come to be aboard the *Trevessa*?" Merry pressed. "You weren't on the crew or passenger manifest. Stowaways can go to prison. That's why we hid you from the crew of the *Trevean* – to keep you safe – and why I told the Customs officers that you were my niece. I will tell no one, but I need the truth."

I lifted my head but kept my gaze on the reddish-brown timber surface – the same colour as the floorboards beneath the table. "A man helped me. William. William McGregor.

He promised to take care of me. To make a home for me." I met her eyes, to show her the truth in my words. I had no need to lie about William. He was a good man and I hadn't killed him.

Merry's sweet smile seemed to warm me from within. "Then I'm sure he'll cross the ocean to find you, when he can. He'll need to recover from his ordeal and he'll take the first ship back to Fremantle when he finds out that you're alive. We must send a cable to him to tell him the good news. They're expensive, though. I don't have the money for it, but if you sell these, you should have enough to send a message…" She reached behind her head and undid the clasp on the pearl necklace she'd worn to church that morning. The strand dropped neatly into her waiting hand and she held it out to me.

"No," I said, pushing it away. I couldn't take her prized pearls. She had given me enough. More than I could ever repay. This would place me even deeper in her debt. I couldn't accept that.

Her expression hardened. "Did he hurt you? You denied it before, but I saw the marks on your body. You were beaten by a man with larger hands than yours. Is that why you don't want him to know you're alive? Did this McGregor take you by force?"

"NO!" My emphatic shout shocked me. I paused to catch my breath and my composure. "William helped me. He protected me from those who wanted to hurt me. Other men…tried. And failed. On the night the ship sank, there was confusion. Chaos. Two men used it to overpower me. They dragged me into a lifeboat – away from the others. One man…he had a knife. I fought them and in the waves, the lifeboat tipped over and we were thrown into the water. I held tight to the boat. One man drowned." I drew in a breath. "The other…he was bleeding from the blade. Blood in the water summoned sharks. Many sharks. I…pushed the lifeboat over and climbed in while the sharks…the sharks…ate him. When daylight came, I looked through the lockers, to see if there was anything left for me to eat or drink. I found milk and a sail, then I slept. And the *Trevean* found me." I closed my eyes tightly. "William saw the boat tipped over. He saw the sharks. He wanted to come to my aid, but the captain and crew held him back. He would have died if he had. He will not come looking for me because he believes that I died that night. Your money will be wasted and your message will not work, for he will not believe it. The Maria he knows didn't speak enough English to send such a message. He must see me to know I live."

"Sell the pearls and send the message," she urged. "Please, for me. Tell him to come to Fremantle so he can see you again." Merry pressed the pearls into my hands, still warm from her skin.

I wavered as the desperation in her eyes touched my heart. She wanted our story to end happily, when shipwrecks never do. I knew this better than anyone.

"All right. But I'll pay you back for this, I promise. I cannot take more of your charity, Aunt Merry. I'll work and earn the money to repay you for your kindness. While I wait for William to come for me."

She bowed her head. "I understand. But what will you do? What work do you know?"

"I know fish and I know the ocean. That is all," I said forlornly. For all my hopes, I already felt lost. Her world was still painfully new to me.

"I think I can help you find a job. A job for a girl who knows fish and the ocean. But you will need a name. Your father's, your husband's…as I am Meryl D'Angelo, you must have a last name, too."

"I can't tell you," I replied. "I'd hoped…"

She laughed. "Speranza. Hope in Italian. If you won't tell me your real name, you will be Maria Speranza, the young fisherman's widow who lives in hope." She shooed me toward the door. "Go now, get a good price for my pearls and send the telegram. The sooner he hears you're alive, the sooner you'll be in his arms again." She squeezed past me, pulling on her gloves before donning a hat. "I need to speak to some friends to see if they can help you." Merry hurried out the front door.

I had a goal, a hope for the future. And a name to go with it. Maria Speranza, the widow who lived in hope.

And for the first time, I did.

Three

A bell jangled as I entered the pawnshop. The bespectacled woman at the counter squinted at me, her eyes flicking up and down my body as if assessing me for sale. She seemed fixated by my bare feet.

"It's Sunday. We're closed," she announced.

Something in the way her eyes wouldn't meet mine told me she was lying.

"But I must trade these for money today," I

replied, placing the pearls on the counter before her.

She picked up the necklace and scrutinised the clasp. "Where did you steal this?"

"I did not —"

"Hold your tongue or I'll call the police. They'll arrest women just as easily as men — especially for stealing something as valuable as this. Any job is better than gaol — even yours."

Mystified, I asked, "My job?"

"You might be wearing a dress instead of just your underthings, but I can tell one of the whores from The Palms no matter what she's wearing. No self-respecting woman would go out without shoes, gloves and a hat, nor without her dress buttoned up properly so her bosoms aren't showing."

I glanced down. The buttons over my breasts had indeed come undone and I fumbled to fix them.

"I don't know what could drive a girl to sell her body, but it's honest work that won't land you in prison, girl. You're safer on your back, earning enough money to live until you can find a lonely, single man who can take you away from such a life. Other girls have done it. Stealing things that don't belong to you will send you lower than you are already. If you ever want a respectable life, take those back where you got them and get back to the whorehouse before the Madam wakes up and finds you gone." She pushed the pearls back to me and pointed out the door.

More confused than ever, I stumbled out of the woman's shop and into the street. The Palms was some sort of hotel with red lights where there appeared to be a party every night. The women who attended these parties seemed to enjoy draping themselves over the male guests. I hadn't seen anyone express this sort of familiarity anywhere else in Fremantle — in fact, people barely seemed to touch in public at all.

I walked to the corner and turned onto Bannister Street, where The Palms was. There were no red lights on now; the place was surprisingly quiet. I stood on the cold paving outside, wondering why the pawnshop woman had sent me here.

"Are you looking for a job?"

A woman stepped out of the shadows on the veranda, smoke trailing up from her cigarette as it shed ash on her stained corset. She looked expectant.

"I am," I began cautiously, "but I –"

"Maria!" Merry's voice startled me. "What are you doing in Bannister Street? Come quickly, before someone thinks you're one of their ladies of the night. What would your sweetheart say if he thought you were selling your body?"

Selling my body? What in water would anyone want my body for? I stared at the corset-clad woman and realisation dawned. These women sold their affections to the male patrons of the hotel. There was no love between them.

I inclined my head to the smoking girl. "I am sorry. My…my aunt is calling me."

She waved as I hurried up the street to Merry.

"I've found a job for you," Merry said as soon as I stepped into the sunshine on Pakenham Street. "One of the fishermen's wives is due to have her first baby soon and they're a hand short in the market. They need someone young and strong who knows numbers and fish. Do you think you can sell fish, Maria? Tell the difference between one fish and another?"

I nodded and smiled. "I believe I can."

"Did you send the telegram to your sweetheart?" Merry asked.

I fingered the necklace in my pocket, unsure how to explain my confusion to Merry. "Yes," I lied instead.

"Good. I'm sure it'll seem like no time at all until you see your sweetheart again." She led the way back to her house. "I hope you like fish. Part of your pay will be in spare fish at the end of the day. I admit I'm quite fond of fresh fish."

I followed silently, stroking the string of pearls across my palm. The warm nacre was hard against my cool skin. No pawnshop nor jeweller would see these. I'd hide them in my room until I could return them to her. I'd earn the money myself before spending any on the search for William. One day, when I'd earned enough, I'd return the pearls to Merry and say I'd bought them back from the pawnbroker. She need never know.

Four

The scrape and clink of my bicycle sounded very loud in the darkness. The only other sound was the swish as the waves stroked the river bank, somewhere to my right. It might be the early hours of the morning and dreamtime for most people, but the fishermen had been out most of the night and when they landed their catch, my work day began.

Leaning my bicycle against a boatshed,

where at least a dozen others would join it before dawn, I smoothed my skirt as I strode down the jetty to the fish market, where no one seemed to sleep. Waves slapped the underside of the boards – the tide was higher than usual, or perhaps the weather was just rough. Not unusual for the middle of winter, after all. The smell of salt was strong, but the stink of fish gone bad was stronger – and the sleepy seagulls lining the boatshed roof knew exactly what it meant.

The fishing fleet was home early. Our fishermen worked in all weather, except the worst. When they sought shelter in the harbour, there was a big storm coming and they wouldn't be going out again for a few days.

A gust of wind almost blew me against the boatshed, showering me with salty spray. Must be some pretty huge waves for the spray to travel this far over the breakwater, I reflected, shoving open the market hall door.

Inside, men carried baskets of fish to the

wooden counters where they were being sorted and graded. Their chaotic movements, dodging in and out of each other's way and around the counters, resembled the frantic fish swimming in the live water-wells in some of their fishing boats. Hunters moving like prey. I didn't bother to hide my smile – they all knew me well enough to know that such an expression was never far from my face. "Good morning!" I called, repeating the greeting or reinforcing it with a wider smile and a nod to each man I passed.

"You look fresher than this morning's catch, Maria. How long have you been working here – two or three weeks, surely?" asked Angelo Lacava.

I inclined my head. "Three years and three weeks, more like, but you've given me the same compliment every morning, so thank you, once again." Three years and three weeks of trying to forget William, wishing he'd come to claim me and knowing he wouldn't.

He grimaced. "You tell Basile you don't

want to work for him any more and come work for me instead."

"You're not stealing our lady of the sea, Lacava!" Tony Basile called, grinning. "Besides, the boys brought in a surprise this morning. I've been keeping it just for her." He lowered his voice. "I told them to leave it in the well so you can see it alive. The boys don't know what kind of fish it is – let's see how good you are."

I winked. "You haven't caught me out yet, Tony. I know my fish. After a long night of fishing, some of you boys can't tell the difference between an octopus and an oyster. Let's see your mystery fish."

He smacked a basket onto the counter. "Wait 'til the sun's up. Can't see a thing 'til daylight. Can you grade the dhufish? They're the last basket left. I had the boys put away a big one for you. He'll keep on ice until you go home."

Merry and I couldn't eat two fish in one day – especially not if one was a big dhufish. I smelled something fishier than the scaled bodies I was sorting. "Why are you trying to tempt me with extra fish, Tony? What are you hiding behind that juicy dhuie?" I lifted a particularly large one and pointed its pouting lips at him.

"Dad wants to go fish up north at the Abrolhos. He says the weather's better and the fish are bigger. But if we go and you work for someone else, you might not come back to us when we return and I…I'll miss you, Maria. Just the thought of you working for someone else makes me want to punch something."

I moved the fish just before his clenched fist hit it. "You get jealous just thinking about me touching some other man's…fish?" I teased.

Tony reddened. "Not just his fish," he muttered, lifting the empty basket onto his shoulder as I tossed the fish into their respective buckets and tipped ice over the top.

Shaking my head, I checked that all our stock had enough ice and crossed to Paolo's counter, which was piled high with fish. "Need a hand?"

He looked at me as if I was his saviour – but one he didn't want to accept. "You know you'll only get in trouble if you help me. I haven't been fishing as long as the others, is all. One day I'll be able to sort as fast as the Basile boys, but until then…" Paolo sighed heavily.

"Got enough ice?" I peered under the counter. "Looks like it." I raised my voice. "You're all in early this morning. Who else is finished sorting and has time to help Merlino?" My eyes swept the men who'd stopped to stare. "C'mon, boys. Am I the only one here with the balls to help a new fisherman sort his catch? If he sells snapper at the price of sardines, we'll have everyone wanting cheap fish tomorrow!"

Three men who'd been talking quietly until I spoke ambled over, followed by two more. It took us twenty minutes, but we had Merlino's catch graded before the restaurateurs and shop owners arrived for the first pick of the morning's catch. I thanked each and every one of them, echoed by Merlino's equally fervent gratitude, and returned to the Basile counter just before a windswept, grumpy Tony reappeared.

"It's blowing a gale out there already and the clouds are black," he said, shaking his head. "I had to check the boats were tied up securely. I've never seen weather this bad in Fremantle before. God knows what we're in for. I've heard of cyclones up north – can't be much worse than this."

I bit my lip. "Cyclones sink fishing boats, even when they're tied up." I turned away and busied myself checking the ice levels, knowing I didn't need to.

Tony hadn't moved, but I could hear him cursing quietly under his breath. "I'm sorry, Maria. I didn't mean to remind you. Fishing's a dangerous job and it's claimed the lives of good men. The sea's a cruel, jealous mistress." He touched the wood counter, as if trying to negate his curse.

I nodded and rose. Wind whirled into the building, heralding the arrival of our first customers of the day.

Five

Despite the storm outside, we did brisk business all morning and I found myself sagging by early afternoon. Fortunately, the last customers were on their way out. An unfamiliar young man now stood behind Paolo's counter, speaking to a girl I recognised. Lucy hefted her purchases and carefully made her way out the door.

I helped Tony search the remaining buckets

of ice for saleable or edible fish, but we had surprisingly few left. People had come to buy their Friday fish early, I assumed, knowing no sane fisherman would go out in this weather.

Laying the remaining dozen fish beside the last bucket of sardines, I heard a high-pitched scream outside. I broke into a run and made it through the doors first. Lucy stood on the jetty, a hessian bag on the boards at her feet. It looked suspiciously empty. "What happened?" I asked.

"Mum wanted some crabs to steam for dinner tonight, so I bought some. One ripped his way through the bag and they all took off into the water! What'll I tell Mum now?" She burst into tears.

I peered over the edge, into the waves. I caught a glimpse of what looked like a claw waving and slipped out of my shoes. Swearing I'd set a bucket of the clawed beasts on the idiot who'd sold her crabs without securing their claws first, I dived into the wintry water after her escaped dinner.

The cold came as a shock, but the push and pull of the storm surge felt far more powerful. I wished I could stay and swim in it for longer, but I'd have to wait. I spotted a swimming crab, then two more, all headed for the shelter of the mud at the base of the moorings. The nearest was currently occupied by a boat with a well of salt water in the middle, which I recognised as Tony's *Star*. Inside the well, a sleek, striped body swam furiously in circles. Mesmerised, I felt my mouth water at the thought of the wahoo. I hadn't tasted one since the day I'd last seen William.

Crabs, I reminded myself. First, I had to catch the errant crustaceans and then I could take my fish prize home. I scooped them up, warning them to keep their claws to themselves, and headed for the surface. I scaled the ladder and dripped along the jetty, not pausing to grab the ruined bag from Lucy's feet. I didn't need such flimsy protection from their claws. No, someone would soon need protection from me.

The wind chilled my skin through my soaked dress, but my body was fuelled by fury as I stormed back into the markets. "Who sold these to Lucy?" I thundered, waving my crustacean catch above my head. "Who thought it'd be funny to give a teenage girl crabs in a hessian sack that they could rip through with their claws?"

"She wanted crabs, so I gave them to her," an unfamiliar voice drawled. "No one told me I had to gift wrap them. Not my fault she didn't bring something better to put them in."

Paolo edged away from his new offsider, shaking his head as he said, "I didn't know. I should have checked. He said he knew what he was doing…"

I nodded to Paolo to indicate I understood, before glaring at the new man. "Idiot. What's your name?"

"I don't take orders from some girl." Idiot strode across the floor to me, wagging his finger to emphasise his words. "You should be at home, cooking and cleaning for your husband, waiting for him to come home and put you in your place, not trying to do a man's job." The wagging finger touched my breast.

I took a deep breath and looked down. The idiot had balls and a growing bulge to match. Not for long. I jerked my knee up and heard him emit a satisfying squeak. Then I kicked his legs out from under him and dropped him to the boards, hearing the breath whoosh out of his lungs as he landed in the puddle at my feet. I dropped the crabs on his chest, where they promptly raised aggressive claws. I hoped they drew blood before someone bothered to rescue him.

"Get her your three biggest, well tied, and give her his share of the catch for today," I instructed Paolo, who nodded and headed past his prostrate employee.

"I'm sorry, Maria," he said sorrowfully. "His name's Giorgio. I needed help and I don't have any family here, so I had to hire an assistant. I was desperate."

He might be more helpful carved up into

fish bait, I thought but didn't say. Paolo seemed to be thinking something similar.

I nodded again and grabbed my coat. I didn't want to wrap it around my soaked dress, but I had little choice. Judging by the torrential rain sheeting down over the ocean, my coat wouldn't remain dry for long, anyway. Yet another reason to pedal home faster. I grabbed the bucket of sardines and tucked my enormous, newspaper-wrapped dhufish under my arm. As I passed Idiot – Giorgio, I reminded myself – I selected a small sardine and dropped it on his chest, just below his chin. His crab colony crowded closer, eager to investigate. "Next time, I won't just kick. I'll cut it off and use it for sardine bait."

Several men sniggered. I acknowledged them with a small smile and wished them all a good day.

"Wait!" I heard Tony call. I halted as I heard his running footsteps, using the spare moment to slip my boots back on. "I'll run you back in the truck. I have deliveries to make, you're drenched and I still haven't shown you the surprise fish the boys kept for you!"

I agreed and followed him to the *Star*. He held his hand out to assist me aboard, but I just grinned and leaped, as always. For a moment, I stood on the tiny deck and closed my eyes, feeling the boat move beneath me in the stormy waves. I could've been on a raft or lifeboat, adrift on the Indian Ocean again, wondering if I'd ever see another soul again and whether my heart would truly break apart within my chest from the loneliness.

"Who was that bitch? When I speak to her father, she'll get the hiding of her life!" I heard Idiot say inside the market building.

He was greeted by silence.

"Get up, boy," Giuseppe Arena grunted. The gruff voice of the grandfather of the fish market was unmistakeable. "You'll do no such thing. If you want to work here, when you see her again, you'll beg Mrs Speranza to forgive you for the insult. And if she says your name is Idiot, you may as well forget whatever you were baptised."

I heard spluttering, followed by a shaky, "What? That harpy has a husband? My God, how does he tolerate her without beating her?"

"Had, boy. He was a fisherman and he drowned in a cyclone up north, leaving her a young widow. And she's Merry D'Angelo's niece. Every man among us would fire you and take Maria in your place in a heartbeat. She knows her fish better than any man alive, handles a boat better'n most and she's a damn good cook, too. A true lady of the sea is our Maria and if she says you're bait, none of us will argue."

"Maria? You make her sound like some sort of saint. Did you see what she did to me?"

"Mrs Speranza to you, boy, until she says otherwise. Yessir, every man here saw you knocked down by a girl. You'd best pray she doesn't do it again, for hell has no fury like that woman when she's angry."

Idiot didn't say any more.

Tony's voice cut through my distraction.

"Uh, Maria?"

I opened my eyes and followed Tony's gaze to the angry wahoo, racing around the circular well like a motorcycle at Ascot race track. I itched to race the fish in open water, though I knew it was far faster than I.

"The boys thought it was a tuna, but it's too skinny," Tony continued. "I thought it was a mackerel from up north, caught up in the storm, but the head doesn't look right. What do you say?"

I grinned. "This is my favourite fish in the whole ocean, and one of the fastest. It's a wahoo, because that's the sound of a fisherman cheering when he catches one." I dropped my coat on the deck, beside the rest of my things, then slid into the well with the wahoo. The fish slowed down, rubbing its smooth scales against my leg as it passed me. I floated, motionless, for a few seconds, waiting for its second pass, before I struck. I seized it by the gills and lifted it high out of the water. It fought me, the tail thrashing against my legs even as I held its head above mine, but I held on until Tony found a knife and cut its throat. He took the dying fish from me so I could haul myself out of the well. This time, I donned my coat against the wind and searched for a bag for the fish. I grabbed Lucy's ruined hessian sack from the jetty and wrapped the still-struggling fish in it. Unlike the teenager, I wasn't willing to relinquish my prize.

I hugged my fish in the truck cab while Tony loaded my bicycle into the tray behind us. Paolo's new assistant didn't even cross my mind – I was too happy.

The passenger door opened and Lucy peered in. "Sorry, ma'am. Mr Basile said I should climb in and he'd give me a ride, what with so much to carry. I hope you don't mind." I shuffled further along the bench seat as she climbed into the cab beside me and shut the door. "Thank you, ma'am, for your help with the crabs. Mum usually does all the shopping, but she's expecting another baby any day, so she sent me instead. She says I need to learn if

I'm to get married one day."

"Call me Maria," I said. "How's your mum and dad?"

"Mum's as big as a house and can't do much, so I'm helping as much as I can. I don't want any children of my own. They're too much work!" Her dark eyes popped wide open. "My brother keeps banging on about some birding expedition he wants to lead up north, with this Naturalists' Club he set up a few years ago. He says when I'm old enough he'll take me, but the guano mining islands up north are no place for a girl."

"I'd love to go," I said. Guano mining – what William was supposed to be supervising. The devil's tit, Christmas Island, paradise for bird crap and crabs…perhaps if I could find the place, I could see him again. I'd show him that I, too, had survived the shipwreck that might have killed us both, and maybe, just maybe…

The door slammed as Tony sat in the driver's seat beside me, shaking raindrops from his hair as he grinned. "Ladies, this afternoon I'll be your driver. First stop will be Lucy's house, then Maria's before I start my delivery run. Last run of the week, if this weather doesn't let up." He glared at the clouds as we set off along Marine Terrace.

Six

"So, where do you live, Lucy?" Tony asked.

She laughed. "Mum and Dad's orchards are out in Armadale, but my brother and I are taking the train home. He'll meet me at the station if you drop me there."

Tony turned left sharply, pulling the truck to a halt in front of the station. He graciously helped Lucy down and started assembling her fish, stacking everything up to carry it for her.

She looked worried. "What's that? I can't take all those home! The ice will melt before we get home!"

Tony glanced at me. "Payment for your trouble. Merlino gave you his assistant's share of the catch to apologise for letting your dinner escape."

Lucy shook her head violently. "Oh, no, those are Maria's. She caught the crabs. Please, Maria, you take them. You went swimming in that dreadfully cold water and got soaked!"

The last thing I needed was more fish, on top of the excess I already had. I peered into Lucy's extra buckets — and saw they were all packed with sardines. There must have been fifty pounds of them. Merry's ice chest might take one bucket, but six? We'd have every cat in Fremantle clawing down our door.

In the face of Lucy's desperation, I nodded, then looked away to keep my thoughts hidden. My eyes landed on a sign on South Terrace. Hee Kee — the Chinese tea merchant. I'd promised Merry that I'd pick up some more tea. We drank far more of it with the cold weather and Hee Kee was the only one who carried Merry's favourite jasmine tea.

When Tony returned, I mentioned my need for tea and he kindly agreed to drive me to the door of the shop and wait while I picked up whatever I wanted. Gratefully, I slid from the truck before he could help me down and entered the shop.

I inhaled deeply as the spicy scent hit me – tea of all sorts. Some earthy, some sweet and some so sharp I wondered what they were made from. Hee Kee himself wasn't in sight – just his diminutive wife. I asked for a pound of jasmine tea and she turned and shouted something in a language I didn't understand. She was answered by the deeper tones of her husband, who appeared with a huge tea chest in his arms. He set it down on the counter and opened it.

The fragrance he released made me gasp. Green tea. The scent after a meal with my mother and sister. Sharing tea with William on the *Trevessa*, when I first told him about Giuseppe. This scent sent me winging home to a past I could never recover.

My reverie was broken by the screech of Mrs Hee berating her husband. The tea box of precious memories closed and he hefted it again. "Sorry, ma'am. Ship delivered wrong tea – strange Japanese tea, not what is ordered. I will find your jasmine tea."

"No, wait!" I had to have it. Memories of William and my family dwelt in every leaf. "I like this tea. How much will it cost?"

Mrs Hee's eyes sharpened as she barked out several short syllables.

Mr Hee shook his head, looking annoyed. "No. I can't ask for more than a shilling a pound. My wife says two, but it is easily fifty pounds. A hundred shillings for the chest is far too much."

Both were too much. I didn't have that much money on me – I had two, not fifty or a hundred. Perhaps I could trade some of my fish for a pound of the precious leaves. I glanced outside and watched Tony tapping his fingers on the steering wheel. In the back were half a dozen buckets of…

"Would you take fifty pounds of sardines, fresh caught this morning?" I asked eagerly.

Mr Hee relayed my offer to his wife, who looked hard at me. When she spoke, her words sounded like, "You new here?"

I shook my head. "No, I'm not new. I always come here for my tea. I work over at the fish market, and…"

Mr Hee laughed. "She said *yu nuhai*. It means fish girl. The Japanese tea is worthless to me – I don't do business with Japanese. But my wife and her mother love fresh fish. Let her see your fish and if she agrees, the tea is yours."

I beamed. "I still need a pound of jasmine for Aunt Merry, though."

He bowed. "I will fetch the jasmine tea. Ask your man to bring the fish in."

My man. I fought laughter at the thought of Tony Basile ever being my man. A good man, yes, but…

Tony jerked to attention as I approached the truck. I gestured for him to get out and help me with something in the back and he jumped to do just that. He carried four of the buckets while I trailed behind him with the last two. Mrs Hee's eyes shone at the sight of the first bucket before the light died beneath her businesslike façade. I hid my smile and waved at the buckets. "Fifty pounds of fresh fish, for fifty pounds of green tea."

Mr Hee reappeared, carrying a second chest. When he opened this one, the unearthly scent of jasmine assailed me. His wife gave him a tiny nod and he set the new chest on top of the old. "Fifty pounds of fresh fish is worth twice that weight in tea. One chest of green tea and one of jasmine. My mother in law and my wife will love me tonight and all week, so thank you, fish girl."

I laughed and uttered my own thanks as I followed the two men back to the truck. Mr Hee loaded my chests into the back under

Tony's supervision while I climbed back into the cab.

Tony started the truck again and we were soon headed toward the river and my house.

Rain drummed on the truck roof and cascaded down the windows as we trundled along, but Tony was strangely silent. It wasn't until he stopped the truck that he spoke. "There's nothing you wouldn't dare, is there? I mean, today you helped one of the new fishermen and had rival fishermen working together. Then you dived into the storm-tossed harbour for three measly crabs and knocked a man down for insulting you. You caught that six-foot fighting fish by hand…and you just managed to bargain down a Chinaman…no, a Chinawoman…for a hundred pounds of tea you didn't have to pay for. Maria, you scare me."

I laughed easily, but I felt a frisson of fear at the sound of so many remarkable things in one day. "It's been a very busy day. It's a good thing the storm will give me a day of rest tomorrow. I shall need it."

"Would you come fishing with me tomorrow?" he burst out.

I laughed harder. "The whole fishing fleet's securely tied against the terrible storm coming in and you want to go out fishing in the middle of it?"

He smiled weakly. "My dad tells this crazy story about how he and his mate went out in a storm like this one in a dinghy. They just sat off the rocks near Cape Peron and fished up hundreds of snapper. He said it wasn't just there — any rocks in shallow water. The snapper go crazy in storms and come right in. The other boys think I'm mad for believing him, but he swears it's true. Between the two of us, we could handle the boat, and we'd stay close to shore. Please?"

Was he reading my mind, my desire to feel the storm's power on the water, instead of holed up in my house? "Come by my house in the morning to pick me up. If the weather's not too crazy, I'll come with you."

"YES!" He jumped out of the truck and cheered, despite the rain running down his face. Shaking my head, I headed for the veranda as he unpacked my things from the back of the truck.

Seven

"How was work? I hope you brought some more tea. The girls were quite a handful today – it seems the storm's stirred up more than the river and the ocean this week. I'm afraid I've had a whole pot since I came home." Merry sat at the kitchen table, behind her empty teacup, looking as exhausted as I felt.

I grinned. "We have a treat tonight. A big dhufish and a wahoo – compliments of the

Basile boys." I laid my bounty on the table and unwrapped them.

Merry eyed the striped fish, its tail twitching over the side of the table even as its pointed snout lay on the other edge of the timber surface. "Are you sure you can eat this? It looks like one of those Tasmanian tiger things, but a fish."

"Aunt Merry, this is the tastiest fish in the sea and it's been three years since I've seen one, let alone eaten one. I'll pop the dhuie in the ice box for tomorrow or Friday, but I'll cook this one for dinner myself if I have to."

Heavy boots sounded on the boards as Tony entered the kitchen, burdened by both tea chests. "Where do you want these, Maria?"

I pointed to an empty corner of the kitchen that Tony quickly filled with my tea.

"Where did you get so much from? We can't drink all that — it'll take us months!" Merry exclaimed, squinting at the chests. "At least you got the right kind, but what's this one? I don't recognise the writing."

Tony leaned against the wall, grinning. "Your niece went for a swim in the harbour today, which caught her a bumper catch of Fremantle sardines. They just happened to be the tea merchant's wife's favourite, too, so she traded them for enough tea to last you until next year. At least tea keeps better than fish!"

I reached for the empty tea tin. "Would you like a cup, Tony? Seeing as we have so much to spare and you carried it in."

"I'd love one," he replied, watching me as I bent to fill the tin from the chest. "That does look good."

Blushing, I straightened, recognising the hint of lust in his expression. Whether it was my still-damp skirt and bloomers clinging to my bum or my naked enthusiasm for the smell of tea leaves, I didn't know, but it certainly put Tony's comments about other men's fish in context. I busied myself with the kettle, teapot and other tea-making paraphernalia in an effort to avoid meeting his eyes.

"You should stay for dinner, Tony," Merry

suggested. "After all, we can't eat all of this huge fish by ourselves."

"Speak for yourself," I said, pouring steaming water over the leaves. "If it takes me every meal for the next three days, I'm not letting a bite of this beast go to waste." The awkward silence behind me forced me to turn and add, "But Tony helped catch this monster and he was kind enough to let me have it. You should stay and have a taste, though it'll ruin you for any other fish."

Tony's relief manifested in a smile. "When you have the best, why would you want anything less?" His eyes burned into mine. "I can't stay because I have some deliveries to make, but I can come back afterwards, if that's all right?"

I nodded. "That'll give me some time to fillet this fish and peel the potatoes. Best be here by five."

He promised he would be, then left, whistling. I heard his truck start up and motor down the road.

I grabbed the wahoo. "I'd better do this outside. This is going to be messy."

"When are you going to let your heart love again?" Merry asked.

My mouth didn't seem to want to close, but my voice had died in my throat.

"Tony Basile is a good man and I've seen the looks you get from him and plenty of others – both good and bad. It's been three years, Maria. Don't you think you've waited long enough for your shipwrecked sweetheart? If he hasn't come to find you in three years, especially after you sent him a telegram, don't you think he might have forgotten about you?"

I almost confessed to my subterfuge with the pearls, which I'd had to keep hidden for months before I returned them to her. The fish markets paid well in fish, but even now, monetary reward was minimal. The fishing industry never had been and never would be a source of great wealth. And I'd never sent the telegram.

"Maybe," I managed to say.

"Don't you owe it to your heart and your own happiness to let another man into your life? One who will cherish you the way you deserve?" she pressed.

I sighed. Yes, I'd love to share my life with a partner who was my equal, but the only man who came close was William. I had savings enough to take ship for any port in the Indian Ocean, but I had no idea where to start looking. Besides, my life here was far too comfortable for me to want to leave. I knew people and I had a place here, with all the fish I could eat, tea and, occasionally, chocolate. What more did a girl like me deserve?

Eight

I slapped the fish on the old washstand we kept on the veranda for cleaning fish. The rusted tub at one end served to hold the scales, bones and guts while I carved the once-living creature into something we could cook. The small drawer that might once have held a lady's toiletries now held my prized filleting knives.

When dinner was scaled and gutted, I realised I'd forgotten something. I called to

Aunt Merry, "Could you please bring a dish for the fillets?"

A few seconds later, the door swung open and she set a large bowl beside me. Instead of returning inside, Merry stood on the veranda, shading her eyes as she stared at the river. I turned to find out what it was. Aside from the higher water levels and choppy waves, courtesy of flooding upriver in Northam and Guildford, the only unusual thing I saw was the stationary launch billowing smoke beneath the rail bridge as a train puffed its way across the span. After perhaps ten minutes, the *SS Reliance* emerged and headed for the dock at the bottom of the hill.

The wet weather had dampened the enthusiasm of what seemed like every amateur photographer in Perth and Fremantle. For the last week, the banks had been crowded with sightseers, clogging the road with their Brownies on tripods, attempting to record pictures of the swirling floodwaters. The rain seemed to have washed them all away.

Once the vessel had tied up, the crew jumped onto the jetty and set off home. Last of all was Captain Henderson, who waved at us and ambled up the hill for a few words with Merry. As soon as he was within earshot, Merry called, "Is everything all right with the old ferry, captain? Why did you stop?"

He waved away her concerns as if they were flies. "Nothing wrong with the *Reliance*, Mrs D'Angelo. She's old and reliable, like her name. No, it's the bridge I'm concerned about. What with the flooding and the storm, I thought I should check that it's still sound. There's a small crack in the abutment, but I'll speak to the fettlers in the morning to see it fixed. Nothing to worry about. That bridge is older than my boat and built by convicts – of course it's showing some wear." He cocked his head to one side, then the other, peering at my tub full of fish innards. "What sort of fish did you pull out of the ocean there, Maria? That's a strange looking monster if ever I saw one."

I smiled, setting my hand on top of the fish

flesh as I ran my knife up its spine. The fillet came away long and thick – perfect. The only other fish that came close to this was bluefin tuna and that was a poor comparison. "This delicious beast was a wahoo. Must've been blown into our fishing grounds by the storm. Now, he's dinner."

He shook his head. "You enjoy your strange fish, ladies, and take care in this storm. Hope the river doesn't rise any more. My wife promised me roast mutton tonight and I've been looking forward to it since Sunday." Captain Henderson rubbed his hands together and set off up East Street.

I piled the last two fish steaks into the already full bowl and held it out to Merry. "What do you think? Fried with a little flour-and-egg batter? Or poached in cream? I have a clove of that Italian garlic Sal gave me last week."

She took the bowl and nearly dropped it, it was so heavy. "How do you normally prepare it at home?"

At home, we ate it raw. I swallowed, trying to decide whether I should tell Merry or lie to make it easier.

Merry seemed to take my indecision for distress. "I'm sorry. I shouldn't have mentioned your home. I know you miss it. The school chickens have been laying far more eggs than the cook uses, so I have plenty of those. If you go pick up some more butter, I'll get these battered and we can fry them up. We could fry the leftover boiled potatoes from yesterday, too – a good, healthy meal. I have nothing for pudding, though, because the chocolate's all gone…"

I blushed. I knew exactly where the chocolate had gone. "I'll buy some more when I get butter." I hurried off to change into clean clothes so I could walk back into town.

Merry's admiring smile made me blush all over again when I returned in my newest dress, one the same blue as today's stormy ocean, covered by my best coat, as my everyday one was still damp with salt water. "Don't forget an umbrella," she called after me as I straightened my hat in the reflection in the hall mirror. I pulled on my gloves and tucked an umbrella into my shopping basket. Though I preferred the less polished look that I wore to work in the mornings, after work I learned to look every bit the lady, just as Merry did, down to the carefully polished toes of my shoes.

Instead of walking or taking my bicycle, I caught the tram to Market Street, where Roma Fruit Palace stood. I dashed through the drizzle to the shelter of the shop awnings and pushed open the door. The delicate chime of the door-bell wasn't necessary – Salvatore smiled broadly, the moment he saw me.

"Good afternoon, Maria. What do you need today?"

"Chocolate," I admitted. "Butter, some more potatoes, something ready-made for sweets tonight, and do you have any cooking apples left? I'm thinking of making apple pie tomorrow, what with the fish market closed for the bad weather."

He laughed. "You need a husband to cook for, Maria. That would soon cure you of looking excited about making apple pie."

"Ah, but I'd have to share my chocolate with a husband," I responded with a smile, examining some tinned goods that I couldn't identify. "It would have to be a very special man for me to want to share my greatest pleasure!"

Sal turned an alarming shade of red. "Well, a husband…he'd give you…he'd share…I'm sure you'd make your husband so happy he'd have no need to touch your chocolate. He'd –"

The crash of a wooden crate dropping to the floor, sending tomatoes everywhere, made him switch from rambling to roaring, "Useless lout! I should have told Mama to send you to America, not Australia where you destroy my shop and earn nothing from your job!" He advanced on his assistant, who was now on his knees, trying to scoop up tomato pulp in his hands.

I pitied the boy and reached for an empty crate. "Here, put the undamaged tomatoes in here and then you can –"

"I don't need your help! Haven't you already done enough for one day?" the boy shouted, jumping to his feet. Between his swollen nose and blackened eyes – none of which I'd given him – I recognised the angry Giorgio. My smile faltered in the face of his fury.

"This is the woman you got into a fight over?" Sal demanded.

Giorgio's belligerent chin rose. "That's the…woman."

"I'd black both your eyes myself if Merlino hadn't already. You apologise to Mrs Speranza and go get her a pound of our best butter. Now!" Sal watched as Giorgio dragged his feet to the back of the shop and out of sight before Sal sighed. "Always was a spoiled brat. What did my idiot of a baby brother get up to this time?" He moved efficiently around the shop, assembling my list of requirements…including an impressive quantity of his best chocolate.

I quickly related the crabs incident and brushed it off as unimportant.

Sal snorted as he placed the items in my basket. "He said he got into a fight for looking at some girl Merlino fancied. Then he said some real unpleasant things about the girl — not fit for your ears, even if they weren't about you. I'm sorry he made trouble for you. My family sent him here to Australia so he wouldn't get into any more strife. Been here a week and already caused more trouble than he's worth. Merlino said he'd use him for bait if he saw him in the fish market again. What should I do with him now?"

"Teach him to help out in the shop?" I suggested. "I'm sorry, Sal, I don't know. Try sending him out on one of the offshore fishing boats that are gone for a while — or pearling. I've heard the pearlers up north are always looking for young, fit men. Maybe if he grows up a bit, he'll settle down." I had no idea if that would be the case — I'd never had much to do with young men at all. It's not like I had brothers or male cousins.

A well-wrapped rectangle slammed onto the counter. "Butter," Giorgio said sullenly.

I smiled my thanks, tucked the butter into my basket, and started fishing through my purse for the correct coins. I was certain he hadn't charged me enough for the chocolate, but Sal insisted he had the right total. Shrugging, I paid him and hefted the now-heavy basket.

"Boy! Help Mrs Speranza by carrying her shopping home for her." Sal winked at me, his open eye showing a fierce glint.

Though perfectly capable of carrying my purchases home, I surrendered my basket to Giorgio, who set off down Market Street as if he knew where to go. I nodded my thanks to Sal and hurried after the boy before he took my chocolate somewhere it wasn't supposed to go. Not to mention my umbrella.

I caught up to him before he hit Phillimore Street, but by that time I was already hobbling and cursing my horrible, heeled shoes.

Appearances be damned. As soon as I got home, I'd make these disappear.

"I live at the end of Tuckfield Street, near East Street," I informed Giorgio. "I'd intended to take the tram home. That's how I got here. Honestly, you could just –"

"My brother said carry your things home. That's what I'm doing." His voice sounded flat and he kept his eyes on the road ahead. We trudged through puddles for a few more minutes, before he said, "I'm sorry I said stuff about your husband. I didn't know he'd…that you were…"

I nodded and kept walking.

"You don't look old enough to be a widow."

I swallowed. "I was sixteen when Giuseppe died. Old enough to be a wife is old enough to be a widow, or so the ocean seemed to think when it took him from me."

"I…I'm sorry."

Silence descended until we reached the gate. I broke it by thanking the boy.

He gave a curt nod and sloped off, scuffing

his shoes on the dirt road as he pulled his cap down.

Nine

When I reached the kitchen, I found that Merry had coated all the fish, boiled some carrots and sliced the potatoes. We were busy stoking the stove, to make sure the frying pan would be nice and hot, when Tony breezed in, carrying a bottle under each arm.

"My uncle's been experimenting with fermenting grapes again. He says it's his best white wine yet, but Mum says she won't have the stuff in the house, not after last time he brought over some home brew that was far too strong. So I saved a couple of bottles for you ladies, to thank you for the meal." He sniffed appreciatively, though all he could possibly smell was raw fish and cooked carrots. "Where's your ice box? I'm told this tastes better when it's cold." I pointed and he stuck one bottle deep inside. "Let's open this one now. Do you have any glasses?"

Merry rummaged through the bottom cupboard of the dresser, moving things around for a full five minutes before she pulled out a strange, stemmed, funnel-shaped glass with a round foot. She produced two more, equally dusty glasses before climbing laboriously to her feet to carry them to the sink. I offered to help, but she refused.

Shrugging, I returned to the stove and dripped some water into the cast iron pans. In the first, the droplets just formed an uninspiring puddle, but in the other they danced on the surface, telling me it was ready to fry my favourite fish. I dropped a generous dollop of butter into the pan and watched it melt and bubble. With more caution than I'd normally give a fillet, I lowered the first piece into the pan, then carefully added five more. Moving them around with my spatula, I decided there was space for one last piece. I breathed in the smell of searing fish and couldn't seem to focus on anything else, until I realised the stinging pricks against my arm were from the boiling water droplets in the second pan. I buttered that one, too, then added the potatoes.

Behind me, I heard the chink and clink of someone setting the table before the sizzling drowned out all other sound. When the fish was almost browned on one side, I added more butter to the pan and flipped them over. I almost sighed in relief but didn't want to show my nervousness in front of Tony. Any other fish and I wouldn't mind, but I'd never eaten cooked wahoo before. It had to be perfect.

A slight touch at my elbow made me jump and almost drop the spatula, but I recovered in time to stop it hitting the floor. "May I try something?" Tony asked. He didn't seem to want to explain further, so I nodded. He tipped the bottle of wine into the fish pan, so that it just coated the base. "My mother swears it's the only thing white wine's good for — cooking fish."

The wine seemed to only enhance the aroma spiralling up, so I nodded again and concentrated on the potatoes, which were just about ready. I took the pan off the stove and tipped them into a serving dish Merry had set in the middle of her best tablecloth. Setting the dirty pan in the sink to soak, I scrutinised the fillets. Almost done…and they smelled amazing. I grabbed a serving plate off the table and transferred each piece of fish over, determined that they should look as good as they tasted.

I slid into my seat, followed by Merry and Tony last of all.

"Will you please say grace, Tony?" Merry murmured and we all bowed our heads as he spoke the words.

When I lifted my head, I found both of them watching me. No one had touched the food. Shrugging, I reached for the nearest piece of fish and deposited it on my plate. Potatoes, carrots and whatever else could wait.

I sliced a small bite off the end with my fork. The flesh was dense and white, cooked to perfection. I lifted it to my lips and tipped it onto my tongue. I closed my eyes, letting the flavour melt on my tongue before I crushed it between my teeth. Oh, it was sublime. Who'd have thought a cooked wahoo could be better than raw?

I opened my eyes so I could see to slice off another piece, only to find both Merry and Tony staring at me in amusement. Tony's eyes smouldered with the same lust I'd seen in his eyes this afternoon. I couldn't fault him this time – I felt the same way about the fish as he evidently did.

"From the look on your face, that fish is heaven itself. I must try some," he said, not taking his eyes off me as he reached for the fish.

Merry was next and the meal seemed to continue normally after that. The Mills and Wares chocolate cake Sal had recommended went down well – and we didn't need to touch my stash of chocolate.

It wasn't until after Tony had left, thanking me for dinner and reminding me about our snapper fishing insanity in the early hours of the following day, that I realised the open bottle of wine still stood on the bench, next to the three untouched glasses.

Ten

When are you going to let your heart love again? Merry's words echoed in my head as I pulled the front door shut softly, hoping I didn't wake her. My bare feet padded silently across the veranda and down the steps. Even in the midnight darkness, the slap of stormy waves on the ferry dock called to me. I wanted…no, I needed to swim in this storm. Besides, I had to check that Tony was right about the snapper – perhaps even find a suitable spot to suggest, when he came for me in the hours before dawn. Until then, I had time to myself – just the ocean and I. Today's swim in the harbour had been too much temptation to resist. I needed to feel the ocean's raw power again.

I stepped off the dock and plunged in, feet first. Cold water caressed me as I peeled my nightgown off and wrapped it around one of the submerged beams beneath the jetty. I wanted no clothing between my skin and the swell.

Stretching, I opened my gills and took a life-giving draught of oxygenated water. It left a thrilling tang of salt on my tongue as it carried away all the confusion of my human life on land. I pressed my heels together and delivered a powerful kick that sent me deep into the channel in the middle of the river. My skin was both warm and cold as it rippled, stretched and covered my useless legs and feet. When I could feel my tail-flukes extending well past the bones of my land-toes, I flipped over onto my back and undulated my way along the river to its gaping mouth, fixing my eyes on the rain-pelted surface above.

I knew when I cleared the harbour, for the sound of waves pounding timber, steel, and stone retreated into the distance and the open ocean beckoned. My true home. Powerful, wind-driven waves stroked my body harder than any man could – even William, when he'd been caught up in our passionate lovemaking aboard the ship.

Much like the time I'd spent with William and with Giuseppe, my love affair with the storm would be short-lived – a brief bout of pleasure before they left me forever, spent or shipwrecked or sent away. One thing the men had that trumped the storm was their ability to kindle a fire in my heart, while the storm left me cold inside. I'd fight the storm to the point of exhaustion, but with men, the pleasure we shared seemed to feed off each other, making me desire them even more.

My heart already loves, Merry, I wanted to say. It loves Giuseppe and William. Perhaps one day it will love another, but only if I know William no longer loves me. I do not forget, nor forgive, but William has never wronged me, no matter what you might think.

A glimpse of a tail smaller than mine drew me out of my reverie. I called to the young dolphin, asking what he pursued. He slowed to let me catch up, then kept pace with me as he told me of snapper schools in the harbour and close to the coast. He'd show me the choicest spots, if I wished, but there were many of his kind there, too. The storm had brought in a veritable feast of fish. I agreed and we swam south, toward Garden Island.

Every rock big enough to graze the surface was a snapper feeding frenzy – a flurry of pink fish, ranging from less than a foot to up to around two feet in length. My dolphin companion darted in to catch a few of the herring-sized juveniles, wolfing them down whole.

"*This is where everyone else is,*" he said, pointing his snout ahead into the churning water. It wasn't hard to see why. A snapper that must've been more than three feet long grazed me as it sped past, closely pursued by two bottlenose dolphins. I bobbed to the surface in an effort to get out of their way. From the crest of the wave, I saw the chimney of the smelting works at Catherine Point, and Robbs Jetty to the south. That placed us at the aptly-named Fish Rocks.

"*Come play,*" the young dolphin said, now surrounded by half a dozen dolphins the same size as he. For a moment, I hesitated, but it had been so long since I'd swum for the sheer joy of it. Especially in storm surge.

Within moments, I was laughing and darting between them, feeling freer than I had in years. It was like being a child again, playing with my sister and the spinner dolphins in the lagoon. Until Mother found out, and then it would be back to tedious lessons on politics, biology, ocean currents and waves. Duyong was the future leader, not me, but Mother had insisted that I learn everything Duyong did, so that I could assist her as she did my mother. But Duyong had died and I was banished – who would my mother make her heir now?

As if my gloomy thoughts had summoned her, she was there. "*You are not one of them,*" Mother said. Her deep blue tail, the colour of the ocean depths, had hidden her until she was almost upon me.

I stopped circling the dolphins and drew myself up. "*What, a dolphin? Of course not.*" I gritted my teeth against the desire to show her proper respect, as my Elder, my Matriarch and the leader of the Indian Ocean Elder Council. When she cast me out, she set me free of her authority. She might rule this entire ocean, but she no longer ruled me.

"*No, not dolphins. Humans. You are not human. In fact, you have more in common with these dolphins than you do with those who are limited to land.*"

"*That is not true. We breed with humans, not dolphins,*" I countered. "*I never heard of one of ours being pack-raped by a gang of male dolphins, nor consenting to such an act."*

A number of dolphins conveyed their amusement at the idea. No, dolphins were not attracted to us as mates, or us to them.

"Do not forget – " she began

"Do not forget you cast me out? Sent me far from home? Stole my daughter from me? Ordered me to find some other man to love, as if that were even possible, after losing the first? You told me not to return unless I could do the impossible. This is me not returning. Making a life for myself here, among people who will accept me as one of their own, though I am not." Angrily, I took off toward the port, not bothering to look back.

I felt the flowing water as she caught up. My mother was old, but her body was as powerful as mine. *"Their people do not swim in storms with dolphins. For all you pretend, you will always be one of the ocean's gift. Your gills and your tail mark you for what you are. One of us, not one of them."*

"They like and accept me. You do not. I will stay where I am happy!" I sped up, hoping to lose her

but knowing it was futile.

"They will learn to fear you if they do not already. You have the power to kill and control many of them — just one of you. Others have tried to live among them and failed. It is merely a trial and it must end. One day you will slip and reveal your secret — and all those you have protected and cared for, you will have to kill. Always it has been so." Her satisfied smile infuriated me.

I stopped and snapped, *"I use my power to help and not hurt them. They are my people now."* The ferry dock was fast approaching and I didn't want to put Merry in danger. Mother's anger rolled off her in waves and all my childhood instincts told me to capitulate and obey her, but the adult in me resisted. I was a child no longer.

She laughed. *"You cannot protect them all. These land-bound creatures and their creations are too fragile…"* She crossed to the far side of the channel and brushed her tail across the sand at the bottom of the rail bridge, scattering sand into the turbulent water. She dug her flukes deeper, releasing more white grains. *"You see what only one of us can do?"*

She'd changed the shape of the sand embankment only slightly, but that was all it took. Knowing ocean currents and their effects was ingrained in me from my earliest memories and my heart leaped into my throat at the knowledge of what her small change would catalyse.

I watched in horror as the swirling floodwaters mimicked her erosion, but on a far grander scale. The Swan River ate away at her own banks until visibility was close to zero and all I could hear amid the swirling water was my mother's laughter.

I stumbled for shore and home.

Eleven

Tony's knocking on the front door startled me out of an uneasy doze. Wishing the encounter with my mother had been a dream and knowing it most certainly wasn't, I quickly pulled on some clothes and ran to meet him on the veranda.

"Did I wake you?" He grinned. "Dad says the weather's perfect. The other boys say…well, I'd better not repeat it. My sister said I'm as crazy as a galah to go out on the water in this weather, though. Are you coming with me to be crazy, too?"

I hesitated. "Should I grab something for breakfast?"

"Nah, Mum packed a proper fishing breakfast for us. Including a thermos flask of fresh coffee, too. After that magnificent dinner you gave me last night, the least I can do is give you breakfast. We'll be back home by lunch, with enough fish to last us until the weather clears up. I hope."

I pulled the door shut as I left for the second time that night, wondering if Merry heard either click. She'd never asked about my night time excursions, so perhaps not. Or maybe she was just so used to me leaving early for work every morning that she didn't notice any more.

Squinting out in the darkness, I looked for the hulking arch of the wooden rail bridge — the one Mother had tried to undermine. To my relief, it looked intact. Perhaps she'd given up and started the long swim home, I hoped, knowing she'd do no such thing. No one opposed Mother without paying dearly for it and I'd paid nothing yet. Nor did I intend to.

"Did you bring the truck, or should I get my bicycle?" I asked.

Tony's laughter rang out. "Neither. I brought the boat. The *Star*'s tied up at the ferry jetty. Just a short walk and your pleasure-craft awaits." He pointed and I saw the outline of the mast against the roiling river surface. Tony offered his arm and I took it for the brief walk down the road to the dock.

I leaped aboard and felt the impact of his feet beside me.

"Oh, look, the dolphins are in the river. There must be good fishing if they're catching fish here." Tony pointed at a gleaming tail breaking the water before slipping beneath the surface.

My blood ran cold, for my sight was clearer than his. Dolphins weren't blue. Mother was watching. "I'll take the helm," I said quickly, moving toward the tiller.

Tony seemed surprised. "You want to be the captain of my boat?"

"Do you trust me to know what I'm doing with your sails?" I countered.

He mumbled something I didn't catch, finishing up with a shaky laugh, before asking me to help him cast off. We were soon underway, slicing through the waves that came to lick the hull before melting away into the darkness astern. As we tacked, Mother kept pace with us easily. I responded to Tony's instructions with the smooth efficiency of a seasoned sailor, for I was. Usually our pleasure-fishing trips had been in daylight on calm afternoons, though.

The waves grew stronger and choppier as we rounded South Mole and passed the breakwater that sheltered the fishing boats and the markets from the storm. The north-westerly slammed into us, sending Tony frantically shifting the sails so he could take full advantage of it.

"Where to?" Tony shouted over the wind. "Running before this gale, we could make Shoalwater and Dad's fishing spot in less than an hour!"

I shook my head. "How will we get back? Beating against the wind? Better to try Fish Rocks, near Robbs Jetty. They must've gotten their name somehow."

He nodded and gave me two thumbs up and together, we turned the little boat to run with the wind. We almost ended on top of the rocks, if it hadn't been for my shout, and we quickly dropped anchor in the lee of the rocks. Not that they offered much shelter from the waves — more insurance that the waves didn't make us drag our anchor and run aground.

"Now we bait up and wait!" Out came a bucket of low-grade whiting, rods, lines and hooks. In the dim light from the lantern hooked to the mast, we baited up the lines and cast them out. Four rods in total — two each, he told me, so we always had a line in the water, even when we were reeling in a catch.

I didn't laugh at his optimism. I'd already seen dolphins popping up for a breath before ducking under again, so I knew the fish were still below us. Enticing them to the hooks was his area of expertise.

It seemed like no time at all before first one of his rods, then the other were bending under the weight of a hooked fish. I helped reel one in as he fought the other and both sizeable snapper were soon swimming in the seawater well in the middle of the boat. Another and another and another…the fish seemed never-ending, until my arms ached from fighting the snapper aboard. Tony seemed to tire, too as the snapper school in the well looked as dense as they had in the water around the rocks.

One by one, he stopped re-baiting the hooks when we caught fish, until all four were out of the water. "Hungry?" he asked, pulling a basket from under the bench he'd been sitting on. We shared sandwiches and hot coffee in silence, lulled by the waves rocking the boat. If I closed my eyes, I could almost imagine I was back in the *Trevessa*'s lifeboat, waiting for rescue and wishing William was with me. Faintly, I heard the memory of the song I'd given voice to in order to help my mind to sleep.

But I wasn't alone tonight. I had Tony.

Didn't I owe it to my heart and happiness to let another man into my life?

My eyes flew open and I regarded Tony's relaxed body stretched out across the bench for all the world as if he was asleep. But he'd just had two cups of tar-black coffee – he couldn't be sleeping! He inhaled in a great, ripping snore.

"He is only a man. While he sleeps, seduce him as you should. Mount him and make him give you his seed. Then you can return home with me and take your place among us again. No one will notice another boat surrendering to the sea in this storm."

The faint singing had ceased and I knew now it was no memory. *"He is a man, but he is also my friend. The ocean will not have him!"*

Mother rested her arms on the gunwale,

cocking her head to the side. "*You think you can protect him? Protect all of them from the ocean's gift?*"

I clenched my fists and stepped in front of him. "*I will try. I will certainly protect him from you. They are not our people, but they love as powerfully as we do. Because they are land-bound, does that make them less than we? They are more numerous and I have heard tales of ships that dive beneath the waves. They will find us, Mother, and we may not survive the battle. Better to slip among them, as invisible as a jellyfish, and take what we need without death. Better that we work with them to protect secrets we hope they never discover. Do not give them reason to hate us, for they will hunt us as they did in the days of dragons and it is we who will not survive this time. Have you forgotten what they did to Duyong?*"

Mother's eyes widened. "*I carried your sister's corpse into the depths myself. I do not forget —*"

"*Nor forgive,*" I finished for her. "*Some of them do not forgive or forget, either, Mother. And some deserve life. They need to be protected from us as much as we do from them.*"

"*If you wish to protect them, then you must lead the*

Elder Council," Mother insisted. *"And you shall never take your place until you obey!"*

"You could do it," I replied. *"You lead the Council. You are its Facilitator and you could persuade them to..."*

"To what? Teach children how to be human? Not to kill? To regard them as kin and not disposable breeding partners? I haven't the heart for such a battle. Especially not after they stole my chosen heir and left me with a disobedient child with a voice so powerful she cannot control it!"

I glared at her. *"I am no child. And I disobey because you are wrong. I will not give the ocean another man for you or for any of the Council. Even this one you cannot have!"* I raised my voice in song, for the first time since I'd arrived on land. Mother might have serenaded Tony to sleep, but I could rouse him. Even as her ethereal tune harmonised with mine, fighting to keep him unconscious so she could persuade or threaten me for longer, his eyelids fluttered.

For the first time, I saw fear in my mother's eyes. *"Come and find me when you find a man you would conquer the ocean to protect. You cannot swim from it. You will be the Elder of the Gold line, and rule the Council as your mother and grandmother before you."* She flipped her tail and dived like a humpback whale headed for the ocean floor.

Tony yawned and sat up. "Sorry, I didn't mean to doze off. Was I out for long?"

I shook my head, peering east across the land to see the faint streaks of pink on the lowest clouds. "It'll be dawn soon. Shall we take our catch home?"

Twelve

Tony stared thoughtfully at the well, where the teeming pink fish matched the dawn-tinted clouds above. "How did we catch so many fish? I don't think I've ever caught this many snapper in a night, not with a full crew and a full night's work!"

I shrugged. "The storm made them crazy."

"Let's stop off at the fish markets and see if we can put some of these on ice or something.

There's no way we can take all of these home — not even with my family. Pity the markets aren't open today — we were the only ones crazy enough to go out last night."

Us and Mother, I thought but didn't say, as I guided us into the fishing boat harbour. A small huddle of people stood on the jetty, watching us as we tied up. I recognised some of the local restaurant and café owners — our first customers of the day, most days. Not today — the markets were closed.

The only fish to be had were swimming inches from my toes, in the well of our boat.

"Tony," I said softly. "What about selling them? We're here at the markets. Those are our usual customers. It's not like anyone else is here with fish to sell…"

As if to illustrate my point, Mrs Davis called out, "What's the catch this morning, Basile? And why aren't the markets open yet?"

"Beauty pink snapper, a shilling a pound! The other boys didn't want to get their feet wet, so they're all curled up at home, out of the storm. These are the only fish for sale at the markets today!" Tony shouted back.

Mrs Davis frowned. "But they were only nine pence a pound yesterday. That's robbery, Basile, and no mistake."

I counted the fish while the two haggled, with help from some of the other customers. I counted twice, but both times I came up with more than fifty fish. Most were easily twenty pounds – some were even bigger than that. A little more complicated numbers work told me our combined catch was worth close to fifty pounds, even at yesterday's prices – a fortune for a day's work.

"Ten pence a pound!" I thundered, leaping onto the jetty. "But once it's gone, there'll be no fish before Monday. Get in quick!"

If business had been brisk yesterday, it blew by in a fresh gale this morning. As the sun rose, Tony and I scooped fish from the well, weighed them and counted coins. By ten, we were down to the last few fish and they were increasingly hard to catch.

"I'll just take the money inside to count it on the table," Tony said, stepping easily onto the jetty and making for the market building. I used his absence to sing the fish quietly within my reach so that I could catch them without having to get right down into the well. I killed them quickly, not wanting to prolong their pain.

Tony returned, wearing a stunned smile.

"How much?" I asked.

"Sixty-two pounds, fifteen shillings and sixpence."

It was more money than I owned — all my savings from my meagre pay to fund my search for William. I grinned. "Your dad will be thrilled. Maybe I can go fishing with you again."

He snorted. "These aren't Dad's fish — nor anyone else's, either. Half of this belongs to you. You risked your life for this catch, too." I realised now that he held not one money bag, but two — and he handed one to me. My jaw dropped. "I'm going to get a second-hand motorbike and take it to the races at Ascot with my share. One of the guys up the road is selling one and I think I'll have just enough. What about you?"

A motorcycle? I'd seen them speed past me as I rode my bicycle home in the afternoons. I wanted to feel that kind of speed and power between my legs. If I stayed here and gave up my search for William, I'd have enough for one of the powerful vehicles. If I lived on land for the rest of my life, that could be normal for me…

"I'm sorry. You must be exhausted. I'm used to fishing all night, but you're not. I should take you home, Maria."

I shook the strange thoughts from my head. "You're probably right."

We cast off and edged around the breakwater and South Mole, into the harbour proper. The going was choppier than the open sea, with the swirling floodwaters meeting the wind-driven swell from the Indian Ocean, but we sailed slowly through the port, waiting for a particularly wide barge to pass beneath the rail bridge before we took our turn. I stared up at the old bridge – built by convicts in the previous century, I'd been told – as a train thundered across it. The bridge creaked ominously and I glanced at the foundations. The floodwaters had swept away most of the bank now – and the timbers visibly sagged as the train gained the northern bank.

The barge had moved and it was our turn to sail beneath the bridge. I looked up and my blood ran cold. A massive crack in the beam above no longer looked like the harmless fault Captain Henderson had described yesterday. Even as I watched, the bridge bowed down to meet us. Tons of timber and steel, coming to kill us. Mother and the ocean hadn't done the job – but she'd left this death trap waiting for me to return home, just in case.

My mind whirled with calculations no human mind could compute – for no human had been trained since childhood to respect the fluid dynamics of current, wind and wave as water flowed over bank and bed. We had only minutes before the water won and this bridge would fall. I couldn't save it. But perhaps I could save some of them.

High up on the northern bank, Captain Henderson and a crew of fettlers carried tools to repair the bridge. Around twenty feet before the bridge started, one of them kicked a stone. The rock careened down the slope, bringing a shower of soil down with it. That was all it took. The crack widened further and for the first time in my life, I screamed in fear.

Thirteen

I shoved the tiller hard, sending us toward the bank as soon as we were out from under the bridge.

"What are you doing?" Tony hissed as the boat heeled over dangerously.

Captain Henderson and his crew stared at me, just as I'd hoped, so I sucked in a breath and shouted, "Don't let your men on the bridge. It's ready to collapse." I pointed a shaking hand at the beam and he slipped and slid down the bank to get closer to us so he could see what I was pointing at. His face paled when he saw that I was right. As if to illustrate my point more clearly, a huge chunk of stone fell away from the embankment, splashing into the river and sending our boat rocking.

"Get everyone clear of the bridge. Someone run up to North Fremantle Station and stop the next train from leaving. I'm going to get the engineers on the *Reliance* and we'll —"

Henderson was drowned out by a tortured scream. The sound a thousand-year-old jarrah tree might have made, knowing it was going to be hacked to pieces and cast into the hell Merry's church priest talked about. Or a beam from that same tree ripping apart under the stresses of storm, flood and too much weight over the bridge built on top of it.

A gust of wind carried the smell of coal smoke from a steam engine, concentrating as it came closer. I turned and saw a freight train steaming along the track on the south bank of the harbour – headed right for the groaning bridge.

Henderson continued pointing and shouting at people on the far bank, but the wind whirled his voice away upriver, where no one could help halt the approaching train. If the train touched the bridge, the whole structure would collapse.

"Tony, we have to get to the dock on the south bank. Now!" I insisted. He followed my gaze to the doomed train and nodded, yanking on a rope so hard a weaker strand would have broken.

We made it to the middle of the river before the sound of groaning timber and stone splashing into the water drowned out all other sound. The northern end of the bridge tore away from the bank and toppled into the swirling waters below, where we'd been floating in the *Star* only moments before. The structure seemed to float for a few seconds, before sinking beneath the muddy waves.

A plank bobbed to the surface, perhaps thirty feet downstream, which was quickly carried toward the ocean and out of sight. Glancing up, I saw that the freight train had miraculously stopped of its own accord. The driver hung out of his window, talking to a flagman. Both were gawking and pointing at the bridge that almost claimed his life. And mine.

Shaking and numb, I helped Tony tie up at the dock. In yet another first, I allowed him to assist me out of the boat. He pushed his way through the crowd of sightseers – armed with cameras again, as if they knew what was going to happen. But they couldn't have, I reasoned. If anyone had known, that last train would never have crossed the bridge. I followed close behind him.

A resounding crash of steel on stone made me flinch, followed by a second. Tony turned his head to look, but I kept my eyes firmly on Merry's house ahead. "What was it?" I asked dully.

"The fettlers' sheds. Where they keep their tools for fixing the bridge. Kept, now they're gone. All washed down the river to the sea now." He laughed. "Maybe the fish will fix it and use it on the seabed."

I smiled wanly at his joke and continued trudging up the hill. If I stopped, I'd fall to the ground and cry.

Merry stood on the veranda, but she was so intent on the bridge that she barely noticed us until we stood beside her. "Oh, my," she cried. "You've just missed the most horrifying thing I've seen all year. The rail bridge collapsed!"

Tony grimaced. "We know. We were the last boat to ever sail under it. It came down just after we were through."

Merry dragged her eyes from the bridge to us, concern in every muscle. "Are you all right? Are you hurt? Oh, I hope no one was hurt. A train had just steamed across the bridge, too — I heard it just before all the screeching."

"No, we're fine. The bridge missed us and there was no one on it when it broke."

My mouth was too dry to speak, so I just nodded slowly as Tony told the story.

"It's a miracle no one was hurt!" Merry insisted. Her hand fluttered over her heart.

Tony glanced at me. "No, not a miracle at all. It was her." He jerked his thumb at me. "While we were under the bridge, she saw the damage and told one of the rail workers up the top. They had time to stop the trains and get everyone off the bridge before it fell. And then Maria insisted we had to come to the dock. If we'd stayed where we were, the whole bridge would've come down on the *Star* and smashed it like so much kindling…"

"I'll go make some tea, shall I?" Merry said, not waiting for an answer. I followed her inside, but Tony stayed on the veranda, watching the disaster unfold further.

Instead of helping her, like the vague voice in my head said I should, I sank onto a kitchen chair. I wanted to be hugged and held and told that I was all right. Like William had. He would have warmed my heart with his reassurance as he warmed my body with his. Instead, Merry silently set a cup of tea on the table beside me and carried hers and Tony's out to the veranda.

Neither of them had touched me. Both were kind, demonstrative people – I'd seen them hug and kiss others. But never me. It was as if a cold distance separated us.

You're not one of them, my mother's voice whispered in my memory.

No, I wasn't. I was me. One of the people of the ocean's gift and I was a danger to the humans around me. The bridge would still be standing if it weren't for me. But had I left with Mother last night, people would have died. The fettlers. The people on the freight train. The avid photographers who even now were climbing over the dangerous remnants of the bridge.

If I wanted to continue to help these people, I needed to choose one to mate with. To love. And the only one I wanted was William.

A cheer rang out from the onlookers outside. I forced myself up from the chair and carried my tea out to the veranda. "What happened?" I asked.

Merry glanced at me and smiled. "The signalmen are trying to keep the telegraph cables from falling into the river. They've rigged up new posts on each bank, but the soil keeps crumbling away, so they've had to move them back already and I think they'll have to do it again soon. One of them hung upside down from the bridge wreckage, like some sort of monkey, and managed to catch the cable just before a steel girder would have cut it in two. Remarkable."

Another beam splashed into the water and two men began weaving an intricate web of rope around a precariously placed signal. A section of the bank dropped away beneath it, but the signal swung away into empty air – and the ropes held it suspended a few feet above the waves. More cheers erupted from the crowd by the dock.

A clink close by attracted my attention. Tony laid my money bag in the tub on the old washstand, giving me a meaningful look. I nodded. He set his empty tea mug on the scored timber beside it. "I'd best be headed home. Mum will be annoyed if the neighbours hear about this before she does. How many of the snapper do you want?"

I stared at him. Snapper? Then I remembered. "We still have yesterday's wahoo and the dhufish. You take them. Thank you to your family and especially your dad for letting us take the boat out."

Tony nodded. "If it's all right with you, I'll leave the *Star* tied up at the dock for today. You'll keep an eye on her, won't you?"

Merry promised we would and we both waved as he headed up East Street, whistling.

That night, as Merry heated up our dinner, I slipped into my bedroom and found the small stack of books I owned. Books about Britain's Indian Ocean colonies. And one small volume written by Captain Foster, about 1700 miles he travelled with William in an open boat after the *Trevessa* sank. I'd read none of them, but now I needed to. And Captain Foster's book I intended to keep for last.

I stood in the kitchen doorway, watching Merry's ever-straight back as she prepared our food. She was old enough to be my mother, yet she had a youth and enthusiasm that belied her appearance. And her eyes…spoke of age and wisdom that even my mother would never have. My short-sighted mother who had threatened the humans I considered my friends. She would not do so again.

"Aunt Merry," I began, waiting for her to glance my way before I continued, "You were right. It is time I let my heart love again. But to do that, I need your help."

"Sure. What do you need?"

Merry was like one of those saints or angels her priest talked about. Always happy to help, before she knew what or why. Even after Tony had told her I had some mystical foreknowledge of the bridge collapse.

I swallowed and set my books down on the table. "I need to learn to read these. I need to know what happened to William so I can find him. He holds my heart, Aunt Merry, and if he doesn't want it any more…"

"Yes?" she prompted eagerly.

"Then I'm going to hunt him down and force him to give it back."

<h1 style="text-align:center">Fourteen</h1>

William's warm body slid over mine, my panting synchronised with his. I kissed him deeply and it felt as if my heart would combust. He tickled my thigh and I gasped, wanting his fingers to travel further up and find…

"Maria, there's someone here to see you."

I swore as Merry's voice dropped me out of my pleasurable dream. I'd fallen asleep in the shade on the back lawn, but the afternoon sun had found me and heated my blood to boiling point. I levered myself up and realised I'd placed my hand on the book I'd been reading. The page now stuck to my sweaty hand. Swearing a little more, I pried it free, only to discover that my hand was sticky from more than my own body fluids. A chocolate-coloured handprint marked the page, beside the plate that had once contained a chocolate bar from Plaistowe's which had melted into a gooey mess in the summer heat.

I decided the book would have to wait, so I reluctantly moved into the shade of the laundry room to wash my hands and, after a moment's thought, my face, too. Only then did I return to the house proper.

The unmistakeable sound of Merry stirring the sugar in her tea guided me to the kitchen, where I found her seated across from…

"Lucy!" I cried in surprise. The teenager had grown up since I'd last seen her, but I wasn't surprised. The city engineers had rebuilt the broken rail bridge in that time and there was talk of building a new road bridge, too, though none of the road boards seemed to have the money to do more than talk about it.

Lucy smiled and set down her teacup. "Hi, Maria. How are you?"

We exchanged pleasantries and meaningless small talk for a few minutes, before Lucy finally revealed the reason for her visit.

"You remember how you were saying you'd love to go birding with me?"

Cautiously, I nodded. Where there were lots of birds, there was guano and the possibility of finding William.

"My brother's organised an expedition for the Naturalists' Club to the Houtman Abrolhos. Dad said I couldn't go at first until he found out that a lot of men are taking their wives so I wouldn't be the only girl there and I'd have chaperones. How old-fashioned!" She giggled. "Anyway, I remember how you wanted to come, too, and you're closer to my age than those old biddies…oops, sorry, Mrs

D'Angelo…so if they get dull, we can go off and have some fun together!"

"I'd have to check that the Basiles can spare me for that long," I began, but stopped when Lucy giggled harder.

"Dom chartered their new boat – the big one, *Stella Maris*. Tony's offered to be the captain if you come along." Big eyes beseeched me, as I imagined they had Tony…and any other man she batted those eyelashes at. "Please come, Maria!"

"You've never seen any of Western Australia," Merry chimed in. "You should. The coastline's very pretty and I've heard there are some unusual fish up there. There was talk of pearl oysters up there, too – a fishery inspector, Mr Saville-Kent, said it was better for pearls than Shark Bay, Broome or even the Great Barrier Reef. He released a whole lot of oysters there, too, but I never heard any more about them. Maybe you'll find some pearls, Maria – to wear on your wedding day."

Lucy both giggled and blushed at this. I

tried not to laugh at the idea. Pearls on my wedding day? If I ever had a wedding day…but if I stayed ashore and espoused a man, I might. Sighing, I nodded. "All right. I'll go. And if I find any pearls, I'll keep them in the hope that one day I'll get to wear them to a wedding."

Lucy cheered. "I'll find out from Dom what you need to bring and let you know tomorrow. It's going to be wonderful!"

She didn't stay much longer, bidding us goodbye and promising to return in the morning with all the details of the trip.

Merry and I waved to her until she skipped out of sight. I looked around for my book and realised I'd left it in the yard, so I wandered around the back of the house to retrieve it. The sticky handprint still marred the page, so I brought the book into the kitchen to see if I could salvage it.

"What on earth have you done to it?" Merry exclaimed.

"I accidentally got chocolate on it," I

admitted.

Merry pressed a cleaning rag to the chocolate and delicately tried to wipe it away from the pages, but only the surface stickiness came away with the cloth – the brown stain remained sun-baked to the page. She sighed. "Well, of all books to coat in chocolate, at least you picked the *Kama Sutra*. What with the number of times you've read this one, I swear you must know it by heart."

I laughed because I knew it was true. I'd thought it a simple book on Indian cultural practices, which we'd used as my reading primer because of its easily read title. As I'd read more, though, some of the suggested sexual practices had fired my imagination. I only wished I had a man I dared try them with. Hence the vivid, erotic dreams that mirrored my longings.

Fifteen

"Heave! If we don't bring that water barrel ashore, we'll have nothing to drink but beer! Think of the womenfolk!"

I heard Tony's unmistakeable laugh in response to this. Probably because he knew some of us ladies had no problems drinking beer. We were outnumbered by the men, so we were perfectly happy to let them haul our supplies to shore. They hadn't even permitted me to row the dinghy in the shallows – though Tony had appointed me his unofficial first mate on the *Stella Maris* for the voyage from Fremantle. Now we were on land, it seemed that Lucy's brother Dominic and his fellow naturalists had assumed command of the expedition.

"We'll be staying in the old guano miners' quarters," Dominic announced.

"Won't they need them?" I asked, looking around. A few sheds, some sort of rusted winch and an assortment of old crates didn't look like quarters for anyone.

He laughed is if it was the silliest question he'd ever heard. I clamped my jaw shut and pressed my hands to my sides to smother my anger. I'd come all this way in the hope of finding a miner I'd been searching for and it didn't look like anyone was home. Nor had they been for years, if the state of the place was anything to go by.

He seemed to sense the danger he was in and decided to stop laughing. He responded,

"No mining at the moment. No one has the capital this place needs and the price of guano's too low to justify the outlay."

I was willing to accept this, so I followed them on a tour of our primitive camp. The firepit and crate seats seemed to be our dining room and the rusty, corrugated iron shed was our hotel. Dominic threw the door wide with a clang and spread his arms in welcome when he walked inside.

Of course, that's when chaos erupted. A storm of beaks, feathers and squawking hid Dominic from sight as the hundred or so birds which had taken up residence in the derelict hut shrieked at him as if he'd invaded the women's changing shed at South Beach.

I burst out laughing and stood aside for the mixed flock of seabirds to leave the shed. When they'd gone, I was the first woman to venture inside.

The birds had left behind a mess of feathers, what looked like a shipload of guano that coated the bunks, table, walls and floor, and a disgruntled community of large lizards, which were making their way laboriously into hiding places. I thought I even recognised a stove under a pile of bird droppings, with a pipe running out to the chimney I'd seen outside.

"Doesn't this look homely," a middle-aged naturalist boomed jovially. His nervous wife crept to his side, peering around as if terrified a bird might come back. "I'm sure you ladies will have it looking immaculate in no time!"

The men's authority over me had lasted a grand total of six minutes.

I gave him a look of deep disgust and stalked out without a word. The five other women – Lucy included – seemed to take no issue with the demeaning task of cleaning up bird effluent and they set to work. The men finished hauling our supplies up the beach and claimed the need to lounge around the unlit firepit with some beer. Tony and two of his cousins remained aboard the *Stella Maris*, securely anchored inside the reef.

Tempted to swim out the ship and stay

there for the rest of the trip, rather than on shore with this depressing drudgery, but knowing it would look odd, I settled for a swim to some of the nearer reefs. I mentioned something to the reclining men about reconnoitring suitable fishing spots and stripped off my dress to reveal my bathing costume beneath.

Feeling their appreciative eyes, I tossed my head and walked into the water. A leisurely crawl in the northerly current soon carried me out of their sight and I dived beneath the surface, eager to see some of the warm-water species I'd missed.

I startled a sleepy hammerhead shark but with a few soothing sounds I persuaded him to remain where he was. He'd surely frighten the others if they saw a shark cruise into view that was longer than the dinghy. Especially if he came from the direction I'd swum in. My laughter bubbled up to the surface and I dived deeper. Most mobile sea creatures had moved away from the large predator, leaving only the stationary ones. And there were plenty of those — I'd never seen so many oysters in my life. The most common was a particularly pretty one with black lips and teeth around the edge of its shell. Some of these let off a slight keening sound that made me want to examine them more closely.

Repeating the same song I'd sung to the sleepy shark, I approached the oyster-encrusted reef. I stroked a keening creature and its shell parted beneath my fingers, showing me the nacreous irritant that caused it pain. Carefully, I removed the hard nodule and its complaining ceased. The chorus of keening from the others increased as if they knew I'd helped one of their number and they wanted to be next.

I rolled the silvery pearl between my fingers, knowing it was bigger and more perfect than any Merry owned. Who knew how many of the precious pearls lay hidden in these unhappy oysters?

I pulled off my bathing cap, shaking my hair

free, and popped the first pearl inside. Then I reached for another complaining oyster.

Within fifteen minutes, the community had quietened and my cap was half-full of shimmery globules in almost every colour imaginable. Blue, white, silver, pink, purple, green…and even a couple in gold. The smallest were less than a quarter inch in diameter, while the largest were almost twice that. Remembering that humans couldn't hold their breath for this long, I surfaced, looking to the *Stella Maris* to make sure no one had noticed my slip. The naturalists, naturally, were still out of sight. No one seemed to be alarmed, so I sank to the seafloor again and tackled another noisy rock.

Bobbing to the surface at regular intervals in the pretence of taking a breath, I slowly filled my bathing cap with pearls. I estimated it was barely an hour since I'd left the party when I sauntered slowly back along the beach, clutching my cap closed in one fist. I heard the pearls click together with every step and hoped that I was the only one who would. I had no intention of sharing my find. These were for Merry.

The men had barely moved since I'd left, I found, while the women were still industriously working in and around the hut.

Annoyed, I marched up to the firepit. "I found a good fishing spot a couple hundred yards that way. Plenty of driftwood on the shore for the fire, too. You have to walk along the reef for a bit to reach the fishing spot, until you come to a blue hole where there's deep water. Some of the fish in there were as long as my arm!" I neglected to mention the sharks that were as big as a boat, for it would only frighten them. Hammerheads didn't like the taste of humans, so what they didn't know shouldn't hurt them.

It was the size comparison that motivated them to sit up and show interest, I believe. Twenty minutes saw them ambling off with their fishing tackle in tow. I smothered a laugh as I hoisted my bag onto my shoulder and headed for the hut.

The atmosphere had undergone a radical change. Far from the flurry of activity I'd seen earlier: every woman fell still as I entered. Two wives whispered to each other and I caught the words, "…lazy, Miss High-and-Mighty, thinks she's too good for us…" as both glared daggers at me.

Daggers? I set my bag on the bunk nearest the door and pulled out the hessian sack containing my filleting knives. I'd supplemented them with a machete, just in case we caught anything particularly large out here. Now I'd seen the sharks and the samsonfish, I was delighted I had. I unrolled the bundle on my bunk, lining the blades up as if to illustrate my unspoken point. I decided to hammer it home.

"I've sent the men off to catch dinner. Hopefully, they come back with some of the bigger fish at the spot I scouted, as well as some firewood. Do any of you have any experience cooking on an open fire? Fish, on an open fire?" Heads shook as I'd expected. "In that case, that makes me your head cook tonight. The stove here is all yours – if you want more than fish, that's your lookout. I don't know what's in the supplies the men left on the beach."

Four of them filed out, moving purposefully toward the supply crates. That left Lucy and I. I searched one-handed through my bag for somewhere to stash the pearls, still clutching my wet cap.

"How did you do that? They've been ordering each other around and squabbling over who did the most work since we got here. Not to mention which was the best bed to claim for their husband..." She giggled. I wondered if she knew what married couples did in bed together. Or I presumed they did, seeing as no one discussed sex at all. Even Merry had blushed when she first helped me read some of the more explicit instructions in the *Kama Sutra*.

I found the hatbox Lucy had insisted I bring

as a specimen case for anything I might find. The pearls would fit in here, but they'd rattle around unless I secured them in something similar to my bathing cap. I had to make sure the girl didn't see them.

"It's about knowing who you are and the power you have, then conveying it through every ounce of your being," I said, translating my mother's often-repeated advice on command bearing and authority. I never thought I'd say it to someone else, let alone a human girl. "And you must meet their eyes, so they can see the sharks lurking in your soul."

She choked with laughter and ran out of the hut.

I quickly tipped the pearls into a couple of handkerchiefs and tied the bundles tightly, before placing them in the hatbox. By the time I headed home, I hoped to fill the box. I'd sell some to a jeweller and give the rest to Merry, in thanks for her kindness and hospitality. Then I would be free to seek William or some other man if he rejected me.

He won't, I told myself. The love in his eyes when I last saw him was unmistakeable, I knew. No. I hoped. Maria Speranza, indeed.

Sixteen

A shrill scream pierced the night. As luck might have it, the source was directly above me – the bunk where Lucy slept. After that noise, no one slept.

I heard the thump of something small landing on my bunk, then the skittering of claws. A stunned rock crab tried to burrow into my blankets. Gently, I pushed it onto the floor.

The second scream sounded a little hoarse. I fumbled for my torch to check on Lucy. In the dim light, she spotted the other two crabs on her bunk and sent them flying to the floor with a well-placed kick.

A muffled male snigger drifted from one of the far bunks.

Lucy's expression slid from fear to fury. She'd evidently heard the boy's laughter, too.

"George Paino!" she shrieked. "I'm going to put these creatures in your bed and I hope they claw off something important!"

She hesitated for a moment, then seized one of the crabs from behind and stormed across the coral shingle floor to the boy's bunk. A scuffle ensued, during which the crab slipped off the bed and sought sanctuary in one of the boy's boots.

It took two men and ten minutes to break Lucy and George apart, though not before she pulled a hank of his hair out.

A number of nervous women started searching their own bunks for crustaceans.

None were found, but a fair few amorous skinks were booted out of bed.

Silence, then slumber and snoring, reigned.

When the sun rose, I slipped out for a morning swim. I was joined by a particularly energetic sea lion, so I lingered in the water for longer than usual. Everyone seemed to be awake and assembling breakfast by the time I returned. I'd eaten a few small fish, but I was ready for more, so I headed for the hut to change into some dry clothes.

A fresh scream set the seabirds on the roof fluttering off in panic. If anything, this was higher pitched than the night-time ones. Grimly, I strode into the hut.

George screamed again, trying to shake the crab off his foot. Lucy dissolved into giggles on the floor.

"Serves you right, boy," Williams grunted from the corner as he tied his boots.

The crab flew, clanked against the corrugated iron roof, then dropped to the floor on its back. A Pacific gull darted through the open doorway, snatched up the crab, and flew away with it.

"You did that to get back at me for last night," George accused, stabbing a finger at Lucy. "Now look, I'm bleeding!" A tiny trickle of blood oozed down one of his toes.

Lucy regained her composure. "I didn't put it in there. It must've crawled in by itself. I'm sorry I laughed at you, but you looked so funny, shaking your leg around with that thing waving like a flag, hanging onto your foot for dear life…Mr Williams is right, though. It serves you right for trying to frighten me. It might've attacked me in my sleep."

Her apology only seemed to make George angrier. "I didn't try to frighten you. I caught them last night and I thought it would be a nice surprise for you to have fresh crabs. I stuck them in a bag and left them on your bunk for you. 'S'not my fault you didn't see them before you went to sleep." He got up and limped theatrically away from her.

Lucy wore a tiny smile. "Wait, stop," she

said. "Let me bandage that for you. Can you really catch crabs?"

George shrugged. "Maybe. With the right trap and bait, yeah."

"Can you show me?"

Seventeen

Every day I breathed the salt air and tasted the tang on my lips, I longed for home. Not Merry's comfortable house, either – the home where I was born. Shallow reefs like these, far to the north. After a week, none of the oysters keened for miles around and my hatbox was full of the source of their irritation. I wished I could stay for longer.

But I was the only woman who did.

The married women had quickly grown tired of fighting the birds from the hut, for the rusted holes in the roof and walls meant they got in, even with the door shut. They'd waged war against the lizards, only to wake up most mornings with a reptilian body cuddled too close for comfort. The water barrel was almost empty, thanks to one of them insisting on washing in fresh water every night. After one woman had seen a shark in the water (and screamed fit to wake the dead, though the hammerhead had no intention of helping her join them), none of the other women would go in past their ankles.

Lucy had warmed to young George and she disappeared with him any chance she got. Her brother eyed them suspiciously every time he saw them together. I don't think she minded the island or the company, but she wanted to be away from her brother's sea-eagle eyes.

The men were divided. They'd hiked out to the wreck of the *Windsor* and taken photographs of them posing on top of the corroded boiler. The fish population had been duly decimated and cooked over the fire. The cameras had come out again to capture the ruins of the abandoned guano mining operation. They'd collected most of the driftwood on the island and tomorrow would have to start cutting wood from the stunted trees. But they were almost out of beer.

The *Stella Maris* was due back today to take us north to the unpleasantly named Rat Island, along with a boatload of supplies from Geraldton on the mainland, but we hadn't yet seen a sail and the sun was close to setting.

When I returned to camp with my afternoon's catch, there were four men lounging around the stacked firepit. I set my gropers on the crate I'd been using as a makeshift filleting table. "Where are the others?" I asked.

"The women went to Wreck Point to collect seashells. Serventy and Sargent went to look at what they think might be a tropic bird. West and Jenkyns took the others to photograph the seals. Williams said there were heaps of them sunbaking on the beach." He shifted the hat which had formerly covered his face. "What sort of fish are they?"

"Baldies. Baldchin gropers. Tastiest fish I've caught this week," I replied. I intended to say more, when I heard a shout from the scrub behind me. I turned just in time.

One of the seal-shooters had evidently found a reluctant subject for his photograph. Williams ran full-tilt out of the prickly scrub, shouting as if all the demons in hell were after him. He wasn't far wrong. Over three hundred pounds of enraged bull sea lion pursued him at surprising speed.

No one seemed to know what to do. The other men froze in terror and I felt laughter bubble up inside me. Before I could attempt to calm the angry sea lion, the creature sank his teeth into his quarry's behind. The man shrieked and the sea lion let go, shaking its head. Taking no notice of the rest of us, the bull sloped off into the water, presumably to wash the foul taste from his mouth.

All hell broke loose as the mauled man's wife was summoned to minister to his bare bum. The sea lion's teeth had barely broken the skin, so the most injured part of Williams was his pride, but he insisted on being treated like a war hero for the remainder of the day.

As I fell asleep that night, I swore that if Tony didn't turn up the next day, I'd swim back to Geraldton on my own.

Eighteen

When I surfaced from my customary dawn swim, the *Stella Maris* floated at anchor in the shallows and Tony was halfway to shore in the tender. I whooped and raced down the beach to meet him, scattering peeping terns into flight.

"I've missed you, too," he called over the water.

My laughter must have woken some of the

others, if the terns hadn't done it, as the shed door swung open and two rumpled men stumbled outside.

It took a couple of hours before they were all packed up and ready to leave. My bag was packed within five minutes and I headed off for a walk with Tony while his cousins ferried everyone and their things out to the boat.

As soon as the others were out of earshot, he asked, "You looked so happy to see me when we arrived. How come you're the only one who's not smiling now?"

I stared at the waves breaking on the reef, wondering how I'd sleep without the ceaseless thunder. Home. It was the sound of home.

"I like it out here. Something about the salt and the sea and the isolation. I'll be sad to go," I said.

Tony folded his arms across his chest and eyed the crashing waves. "Dad said the new boat's perfect for setting up a fishing business up here. We're late because we were checking out the mangrove islands to the north of here

– some look big enough to set up a permanent camp. Houses and jetties out to where the water's deep enough to float even our *Stella*." He sighed. "My cousins are supposed to be the ones to set up the new business while I stay in Fremantle and run the rest from there, but if you like it out here…I'd leave Fremantle to the others and start fresh up here with you, if you want."

His eyes held a serious question and I knew I couldn't just shrug it off. Tony's questions had grown increasingly serious, the longer I'd known him. "I'd love to return here. Fishing out here would be a wonderful life, I think, though not an easy one."

He turned to face me and the look in his eyes smote my heart. "Maria, I know you don't want to love another fisherman after you lost your husband, but do you think that maybe in your heart you might –"

"Tony, you better come quick." Vince Basile burst out of the bushes. "One of the tourists wants to bring a seal on the boat with him.

Says he wants the head as a trophy for goring his leg. Only the seal isn't dead yet and he wants us to catch it for him."

Tony swore in Italian and reluctantly followed his cousin back to the boat. A quick exchange made Williams decide that he didn't need a dead sea lion after all and I realised we were the only ones left – everyone else was aboard the *Stella*. I handed my bag to Vince and helped Tony push the boat off the beach and into the shallows, before leaping in. I took my preferred seat at the bow and curled my knees up on the bench beside me.

Tony didn't finish whatever he'd been trying to say, but he seemed as deep in thought as I was. Could I live out here? Yes. Could I spend the rest of my life operating a fishing business out here? Absolutely. Could I do it side by side with Tony? Yes – we made a great team. Could I love Tony, the way he did me?

If it weren't for William…

I didn't know.

Nineteen

In contrast to our previous campsite on Pelsaert Island, Rat Island was positively civilised. Tony tied the *Stella* up beside a long, stone jetty that jutted out from the northeast corner of the island. All our supplies went into carts that ran on rails to limestone buildings on the island. No steam engine pushed these, though – they were hand carts. It was still an improvement over the rusty hut we'd shared for the last week.

The rattling carts announced our arrival far more effectively than any doorbell. I recognised some of the fishermen who appeared outside the buildings. Lombardi, Davis, Cuocci...and several other men I knew vaguely by sight but couldn't name. Vince, Steven and Tony exchanged greetings with the other fishermen, who fell silent when they saw me.

Silence I felt compelled to break. "Good morning." I glanced around. "Where are the famous rats the island's named for?"

Most of them laughed. The notable exception was Davis, who acted as though I'd offered him a personal insult.

"You'll see them soon enough," Lombardi said. "We have cats to keep 'em down, but even the cats can only catch so many a night."

It turned out that all of the houses were taken by the various fishermen, so we were portioned out. Lucy, Domenic and I, along with the three Basile boys, would be staying in the same one as Lombardi. The married couples went with Davis and the remaining single men ended up in the third building, following a blonde fisherman I'd never met before.

After a lunch of sandwiches made from some of the fresh supplies Tony had brought from Geraldton, Davis insisted on taking us on a walking tour of the island. It was very easy going, as he followed the path of the railway tracks that ran all over the island. Part of the guano miners' infrastructure, he said, when I asked. My heart sank as I realised that there was no mining going on here, either. What if William's mine had closed and he'd gone back to Scotland? I could take ship for there, but I'd spent months learning about the colonies – I knew little or nothing of Scotland.

"Where are the guano miners now?" Mrs Williams ventured.

Davis shrugged. "Doing other jobs, or working at other mines. The new factories in Europe want higher grade guano than we have here. Maybe at Christmas Island."

Christmas Island! That's the place William had spoken about. I wanted to ask more about it, but Davis was already twenty feet ahead of me and I hurried to catch up.

When we reached the southwest corner of the island, I stared out to sea, drowning out Davis' commentary as I listened to the boom of the breakers on a reef I could barely see. Pelsaert wasn't the only island that felt like home – this one did, too. And this one had a water supply – Davis had already pointed out the stone well.

If I stayed on land, I wanted it to be here. Isolated from cities where my people could do the most harm, but still among humans. There were plenty of fish – the large number of fishermen here proved it. Maybe I could build a house here, facing the ocean, and a jetty like the stone one I'd seen. I stepped closer to the cliff, wanting to see how deep the water was here.

"Careful, Maria!" Davis said, pointing down.

My eyes followed his finger and I realised I was treading on a grave. I backed away hurriedly and scanned the marble cross marking the head of it. Giuseppe Benvenuto, who'd died…in the summer of 1921.

No. It wasn't possible. My Giuseppe had drowned and I'd seen his body sink to the ocean depths. It couldn't be buried in the stone beneath my feet.

Numbly, I barely listened to whatever Davis said as he led us around the island, pointing at birds, nests and piles of rocks as if they had the power to interest me.

I sat silently by the fire as others prepared our dinner that night. The stars spilled across the sky like scattered salt and I willed my body to be as cold as they appeared to be. No feeling, no pain.

The fishermen started telling stories of shipwrecks at the islands and I realised there'd been a lot. One where the people had massacred each other when their food and water supplies ran low. One where they'd survived by hunting seals on Pelsaert Island. Idly, I wondered if Williams' bum-biting bull remembered those days and had been seeking revenge.

When someone mentioned that we'd been at Pelsaert and seen the wreckage of the *Windsor*, Davis piped up with the sad tale of how some of the guano miners who'd gone to rescue those aboard the *Windsor* had perished in the attempt and that's why the mining camp was empty – because it was haunted.

Several men laughed at this, but Davis insisted it was true. "There's a vengeful ghost here on Rat Island, too, you know," he added.

He seemed to treat the loud laughter as an invitation to continue. "There was a cyclone that hit the Abrolhos a few years back. The fishing boats were all securely tied in the anchorage here, just like they are now, but one boat broke free. When it overturned in the huge waves, the two men aboard were thrown into the water. It was each man for himself and they both struck out for shore, but only one man reached it – the skipper. The other man – his mate – disappeared.

"Now, in the morning, when the storm had died down a little, the skipper told everyone his mate couldn't swim, so no one looked very hard for the man before they called off the search. Instead, they looked for the boat and brought it up to the surface for repairs. Three weeks later, on the day the skipper's boat was finally ready to go fishing again, the guano miners came back to repair the damage to their jetty and start work again. One of them noticed something strange on the island just to the north of here. Three fishermen rowed a dinghy over to the island for a closer look.

"There, they found the mate's body. He'd hauled himself out on the island with a broken leg, like an injured seal, and there he lay, in full view of the skipper repairing his boat here on the beach. And the skipper just let him lie there until he died of thirst and exposure. Now that's a horrible way to die. The fishermen buried his body at the southwest point, in the grave you saw. So now that vengeful mate roams Rat Island at night, looking for the skipper who murdered him by letting him die slowly for want of a drink of water."

"Davis, you're a damn liar," a voice roared. The man who stormed over to Davis looked like he'd been relieving himself and his pants were in danger of slipping down, he'd returned so fast. "No one ever saw Benvenuto on that island. We found his body down near the southwest point and he drowned, man. I tried to carry a rope to shore to help him, but the current was too strong and I had to let go or I'd have died, too. The last time I saw him alive, he was floating on the well hatch. We searched every damn island twice for him and Little Sandy Island isn't big enough to ignore someone on. I wasn't the only man here. Lombardi, you were here. Weston and Olivari, too. I no more murdered him than you did, you —"

The man with the rope. I recognised him. This was the man who'd almost drowned beside my Giuseppe. The body buried at the cliffs was him. I jumped to my feet and hurried away, feeling hot tears streaming down my face. I didn't care. I followed the tram lines blindly until they ended at the cliff and the body of my beloved.

He'd let go of that hatch to cling to me, so I could swim him to safety. We'd beached, yes, at a deserted sand island that was just for us. And in the cold, surrounded by storm and not knowing what the future held, we'd made love. He'd been a gentle lover, for he knew it was my first time, and I'd responded to his touch as if there were fire in my blood. Fire I could use to warm him.

I fell to my knees on the grave, sobbing my heart out and wishing I could hold him one last time, but I knew I never would. It was my fault for trying to return him to his people. If I'd left him on the tiny island, they'd have found him quickly and he might have lived. Instead, I'd pulled him back into the water to his death. The sharks had come and I forgot he was asleep. I forgot he couldn't swim and his heavy clothes would drag him under. I forgot he didn't have gills and a tail as I did. I'd fought the sharks and I'd lost him. And when I found his body on the seafloor, it was cold. Cold as my heart. Cold until the day William woke it with a touch. And I'd almost killed him, too.

"Maria?"

I didn't want to answer. Maria had been Giuseppe's name for me. I now knew it wasn't that at all – he'd thought I was Saint Maria, Star of the Sea, the virgin saint the churchgoers believed had borne their saviour. He'd thought I was the saint come to save him and not the siren who would swim him to his death. I was safer swimming away. Safer for all those humans I'd hurt if I stayed near them for too long. Time to end this misguided trial of living life on land. I'd failed. The ocean had won as it always did.

I needed to slip over the cliff, into the water and away. But if I did, Tony would follow me.

He'd followed me from the fire and it was his voice asking me, "Maria, are you all right?"

Swallowing, I nodded, then realised that it was too dark for Tony to see the movement of my head. "I just…he drowned in a cyclone." I hiccupped.

"He did. Lombardi helped dig the grave and the boys at the Young Italian Club paid for the marble headstone. He…damn. You're thinking of your husband, aren't you? That's the life of a fisherman. Never knowing if this voyage will be your last, if the next storm will swallow you, or if the fish will bite and bring you enough income to feed your family. No woman deserves to be married to a man who may never come home. Maybe fishermen shouldn't get married. Like priests, only married to their boat instead."

I managed a weak smile. Wearing a priest's robes on a boat was a terrible idea. Not practical at all.

Almost as stupid as diving from this cliff and swimming away from the life I'd built, as if

I could run from it.

"I wouldn't be surprised if Lombardi and Miragliotta stake Davis out for the rats and seabirds tonight. He won't be telling any more scary stories tonight, that's for sure." Tony snorted. "Do you want to go back, or stay out here a bit longer?"

I rose and dusted off my hands. "We should probably go back. It's pretty cold away from the fire with that southerly blowing."

Twenty

"I've never seen pearls this big. And the colours! Where did you get these?" Charles asked as he fingered the globes spread across his black velvet cloth.

I smiled at the jeweller. "Fishing up north, we found some unusual oysters. When I opened them up, this is what I found." What I didn't add was that the handful I'd given him was only a tiny part of what I had at home.

And these were the poorest quality ones, too. In the fortnight I'd been home from the Abrolhos, I'd done my research with the pearl merchants. More than they'd realised – from their ledgers, I knew who paid the best price for pearls and he sat in front of me now.

"I'm not sure I could give you more than a hundred pounds for them, Maria. No one can afford luxuries like pearls nowadays. I'm sorry."

I hid my smile. Davis had tried to offer me fifty and the best offer from anyone else had been eighty. I nodded gravely. "Then I must take it and hope I find some more."

I surrendered my pearls and became the surreptitious owner of ten new ten-pound notes. I knew exactly what I'd do with the money, too. This would pay for my passage to Christmas Island and home again, if that's what I needed. It would also pay for me to live comfortably wherever I found myself over the next year.

That's what I gave myself: the space of one

year to find William. If I failed, then I would come home.

I walked along the quay instead of Canning Road today. Sustenance workers were repairing the road and I wanted to avoid them as much as possible. I recognised and sympathised with the haunted look in their eyes and the sheer desperation that motivated them, but I knew desperation could drive a man to do many things he normally wouldn't. I'd heard stories of theft, assault and other such crimes and I had no intention of falling victim to them. Especially not with an unusually large amount of money in my purse.

I greeted the harbourmaster and asked after the *Islander*. She was due to arrive from Christmas Island later in the week and when she left I intended to be aboard. That meant speaking to the captain as early as I could to make sure I could secure passage with the vessel.

"You're looking at her," he said, pointing at a small, unfamiliar steamer berthed at a spot where I was used to seeing much larger vessels. A man in a captain's peaked cap stood on deck, gesticulating to a couple of lumpers.

I thanked the harbourmaster and hurried toward the ship.

"Pardon me, captain," I called to the man's retreating back.

The two lumpers nodded to me and sauntered off for a smoke beside some large crates on the quay.

The captain stopped and turned, passing a hand over his eyes as if to wipe tiredness away. "What is it, miss? I have a ship to load and it looks like I might have to do it myself. The chief engineer will burst a valve over this, mark my words."

I summoned a friendly smile. "I just wanted to know how long your vessel is in port. I've always wanted to go to Christmas Island."

He burst out laughing. "Miss, you must be talking about some other island. It's a rock full of birds and crabs in the middle of the Indian Ocean. The only good thing about it is that the birds make lots of fertiliser we can mine and sell to Japan. Otherwise, we'd leave the island to the crabs."

"You mean the mine's still running?" I asked eagerly.

He laughed even harder. "Miss, if it wasn't, why would we be here to pick up the new locomotive?" He waved at the crates the lumpers were using for their smoko. "Now I find out there's some sort of labour dispute. I should have brought workers from the island instead. We'll be lucky to head back next week like we're scheduled to."

"How much would it cost for passage to Christmas Island?" I ventured.

"I don't know if we're taking passengers this trip, miss. Ask me next week, when we're loaded up and ready to leave. We might have a spare berth then. Is it for yourself?"

I nodded.

"Then a whole cabin. I don't know." He looked mournfully at me. "Truly I don't. It's a Christmas Island Phosphate Company ship and it's up to their highest ranking employee what it carries. That isn't me, miss. That's the chief engineer and he's the tightest, most miserable bastard I ever laid eyes on."

I wondered how William worked with such a man, what with William's ever-present smile and easy laughter. Maybe the engineer was new and unhappy to be sent to such a desolate spot.

Heavy boots sounded on the deck. "Captain, how long are you granting shore leave for?" a male voice shouted.

"You better go, miss. Find me next week, when we're loaded up." The captain turned and hurried away.

Twenty One

"You're looking lovely this morning. All dressed up, too. You know Sunday isn't until tomorrow, don't you?"

I laughed as Merry fell silent and poured herself some more tea. Her body shuddered as she started coughing again. My chest ached in sympathy for her pain.

"Are you sure you'll be all right without me?" I asked.

She nodded, unable to answer between the barks of her lung-wrenching coughing fit.

"Merry, I don't have to go to the races today. I can stay here to take care of you. I'll even postpone my trip if I have to. You've been so good, taking care of me for all this time. The least I can do is nurse you when you're so sick."

Merry shook her head violently. "No. You need to do this. Find your future. The path you want to travel. Follow where your heart leads, ssss –" Her words disappeared into more coughing.

I grasped her hands. "All right, but you return to bed and rest. The doctor said you won't get well without it."

I couldn't explain how I'd come to care for her more than I did my mother, but Merry's kindness through the years she'd let me live with her meant more to me than eighteen years of my mother's cold community.

The truck engine rumbled outside and I heard male laughter. I rushed to the door, checking my hat in the hall mirror as I slipped into my horrible, heeled shoes. There was such finality in the click as the front door closed behind me.

Tony waved from the driver's window while the men in the cab with him wolf-whistled. The truck's tray was full of fishermen instead of their catch today, all dressed up to go to the races. "Come on up, Maria."

Squabbling started over where I was to sit in the back, while I wished I wasn't wearing a skirt. What I wouldn't give to be wearing practical pants like the men today. Climbing over the sides in this was a recipe for disaster.

Tony appeared at my side. "She's riding in the cab with me. Vince and Steven can sit in the back with you lot."

Gratefully, I took his hand and allowed him to assist me into the seat.

"You look beautiful and you smell heavenly," he said as soon as the doors were shut.

I laughed. "The smell is Aunt Merry's

perfume. She insisted I wear some tonight. Made of myrrh, sandalwood and flowers, she said."

"I've never smelled myrrh, though we get plenty of sandalwood come through the port. Myrrh is something I only hear about at Christmas." He grinned and urged the truck to start moving down the road.

We headed up Canning Road, along the river to the racetrack. The tide was out, so the river mud smelled musty as the morning sun struck it. Behind us, the men were complaining about the smell and blaming each other for breaking wind.

"Have I told you how happy I am you decided to come with us?" Tony said, glancing at me before returning his attention to the road.

We bumped and jolted all the way to Ascot Racecourse. Outside the entrance, there must have been twenty or thirty motorcycles lined up along a line painted in the dirt. The blokes in the back jumped out and I slid down to the ground without waiting for assistance. Steven appeared, wheeling Tony's Indian motorcycle and wearing a huge grin. "With your good luck charm along, you'll have no trouble this time, cuz."

Tony deliberately avoided my searching gaze, so I was forced to ask, "Good luck charm? Are you racing today? I thought we were just here to watch!"

"We're all here to watch," Vince drawled. "But Tony's entered the Half-Day Trial. He's got a lady he wants to impress."

It was on the tip of my tongue to ask who'd caught Tony's fancy, but a quick glance at his blush told me I already knew.

The rest of the morning was interminable, as the race organisers explained the rules, the nature of the thirty-three mile track and how they'd be watching to see how many time the men put their feet down to help their bikes through the various hazards around the track. Tony and his fellow motorbike enthusiasts didn't look anywhere near as bored as I was —

quite the contrary. Every word seemed to increase their excitement about the race.

Noon came and went with sandwiches served in the refreshment tent beside what one of the race organisers informed me was the finish line. He turned out to be Mr Davy, one of the office-holding members of the Motor Cycling Association, and he was soon explaining the difficulties of the course to me and, not long after, to Tony.

I decided to take one more sandwich before Tony turned to me, said, "Wish me luck," and headed off. Past him, I could see the other competitors checking and mounting their motorcycles. Finally, the race was about to start. I crammed the last sandwich into my mouth and looked around for somewhere to sit and watch the race.

"Here, Mrs Basile. Come to the judges' box so you can see better," Mr Davy said.

I almost choked on my food, but my mouth was too full to speak, so I let him lead me up to the temporary judges' box to the sound of sniggers from Tony's friends.

"Gentlemen, start your engines!" someone called. Twenty-six booted feet kicked the starters for the motorcycles and engines rattled to life. Several seconds and a great deal of swearing later, all the bikes were vibrating, ready for action.

"GO!" he bellowed, barely loud enough to be heard over all the engines. Dirt flew and the convoy of motorcycles took off.

A nailbiting wait ensued as the buzz faded even from my acute hearing and all I could hear was the chatter of those who'd remained here to watch the end of the race. Everyone else had headed for vantage points around the hazards. With my best dress and heeled shoes on, I was hardly dressed for traipsing through the bush, so I sat forlornly in the judges' box, waiting for the riders to come through for the second lap.

I heard them before I saw them, but the first two burst out of the scrub and whined around the curve to cross the starting line for the second time. To my surprise, the third man to appear was Tony on his Indian. I cheered and he lifted a hand to wave, though his eyes never left the track. Hot on his heels was a man wearing a huge pair of goggles, hunched over his Triumph.

One of the motherly women who'd brought out the sandwiches lifted a tray up to the judging box. Mr Davy offered it to me and I thanked him as I took the nearest mug of steaming, milky tea. For several minutes, motorcycles sped past us, headed around the track for their next lap before the sound of their engines faded into the distance once more.

When the next wave came through, for a moment I thought it was Tony on the leading motorcycle, but the Sun the man was riding wasn't Tony's. He zipped past, closely followed by another man I didn't know. Tony crested the rise beside Goggles, edging slightly ahead of him to take the inside of the curve to their final lap.

In a momentary lull between a river of motorcycles, Mr Davy remarked, "Your husband's holding his own with some of the best riders in the state, Mrs Basile."

It took me a moment to realise he was referring to Tony – and speaking to me. I blushed. How to correct him without saying the wrong thing? "Oh…I'm not…I mean, he's not…"

My flustered attempt at explaining was drowned out by loud cheering from a crowd of men who'd appeared by the finish line.

Mr Davy jumped up. "And the winner of the Half-Day Trial is…Wilkinson, on his brand-new BSA, followed by Armstrong on his Sun in second place!" he roared.

I heard buzzing in the distance and a third motorcycle appeared. "Third place goes to…Hunter!" Two more crested the rise, gunning their engines furiously to outdistance one another, but neither seemed to be able to lose his opponent. "Fourth is tied – Mortlock and Charman!"

My heart plummeted. Where was Tony?

Twenty Two

I counted the riders as they crossed the finish line. Nineteen, twenty, twenty-one…

"Mr Davy? Basile and the man with the goggles took a tumble on that last stretch in the swamps. Both motorcycles ended up in the river," a mud-covered man said. He tried to wipe some of the muck off his face, but he only succeeded in smearing the mess.

"Thanks, Charman. Were the men all right?"

Mr Davy glanced at me. "Mrs Basile here is worried about her husband."

I gritted my teeth to stop myself from exploding at him. My name and married state weren't as important as finding out whether Tony was hurt.

"I saw Basile start walking back, but I don't know about the other man. Should I head back and see if I can help, sir?" Charman asked.

"I'll go, too," another man offered.

Four riders set off down the former race track, in the opposite direction they'd raced.

I waited. And waited. And waited some more.

A muddy figure trudged to the top of the rise, walking his equally brown motorcycle. "Davy, the next time you let a rank novice join a half-day trial, warn me." Tony spat on the ground. "I'll stay away. Damn near lost my Indian in the river because of that idiot. I think he did lose his, whatever it was. Better off at the bottom of the river than on the road."

Steven and Vince relieved Tony of his bike

and wheeled it over to the truck while Tony advanced on Mr Davy and I. "Maria, you should get one of the boys to help you into the truck. I'll be right there. I just need to speak to Davy for a minute." There was an entreaty in his eyes that begged me to do as he asked, if only this once.

I nodded and headed for the truck. I stumbled as the heel of one of my stupid shoes caught on a tree root. Swearing, I yanked them off and carried them to the truck barefoot.

A strange sound caught my ears, like the creaking of wet leather from the most enormous pair of boots ever made, and I stopped to find the source. The man with the goggles marched down the track toward Tony, his leather pants shining in the last rays of the evening sun. His leather jacket hung open and I could see that his shirt beneath it was soaked, too. It looked like he'd gone for a swim in the river with his bike, fully clothed and all.

"Bloody idiot," Tony muttered and spat at the man's feet. He turned to walk away.

Goggles grabbed his arm and somehow forced him to turn around to face him again.

"Let go, mate. I'm here with my cousins and…it won't end well for you." Tony jerked his thumb over his shoulder at the truck.

Goggles glanced my way and froze. Slowly, he let go of Tony, not taking his eyes off the men behind me. Then he yanked off his goggles, swiped his shirt across his face, and stared.

My shoes slipped from my nerveless fingers and thudded to the dirt. "William," I whispered, but no sound came out.

Twenty Three

Jostling male bodies surrounded me as it seemed like every one of Tony's support crew itched to join the fight against William.

William would annihilate the lot of them. I'd only seen one man best him in a fight and no one else here had the training to match Kaito. They had no idea who or what they were dealing with.

William evidently thought the same thing.

Through the forest of bodies, I saw him walk away.

No! I needed to speak to him. I couldn't let him slip through my fingers like this. I needed to know…

The crowd of men parted to permit Tony through. "Let's go, Maria. I'm sorry you had to see that. I should take you home." His footsteps dragged him to the driver's side door.

I wet my lips. "I should thank Mr Davy for his hospitality." I marched to the relieved-looking race organiser and dropped my voice so the words wouldn't carry to the truck. "Thank you for taking such good care of me during the race. Please, can you tell me where that man lives? Just in case a letter of apology is required."

Mr Davy gave me a conspiratorial wink. "Smoothing things over for your husband, eh? Mrs Basile, I'd tell you if I could, but I believe that the chap couldn't give me an address. Said he was staying at the Esplanade Hotel in

Fremantle for a few days while his ship is in port before he leaves the country. He only joined the race because he said he wanted to try out a new motorcycle to see if it would perform well in the jungle. I hope there aren't many rivers in his jungle!" He laughed uproariously.

I managed a small smile in response and bade him farewell. I padded back to the truck, enjoying the feel of the damp dirt between my toes. Shoes and civilisation were overrated.

Ignoring the offers of assistance, I climbed into the passenger side by myself, slamming the door behind me. As soon as I was settled, Tony rammed the truck into gear and took off in a spray of gravel.

We drove in silence for perhaps fifteen minutes before Tony broke it. "I'm so sorry, Maria. I thought you'd enjoy watching the race and afterwards, I'd planned…I wanted…" He swallowed and gripped the steering wheel tightly. "Never mind. I should've taken you to dance at the Hydrodome instead. I will. I…will you come with me to the tearooms tomorrow evening? We can have dinner and I heard there's a new jazz band playing. Please say yes. I want you to remember me when you're steaming home to England and when you're visiting your mother. I want you to want to come back to me here."

It took me a moment to remember the story I'd told to mask the real reason for my desire to depart. It was Merry's idea, for she was the only one who knew the truth. Who would believe that steady, dependable Maria Speranza would go haring off on a wild quest for a man who didn't know she existed?

He did now. He'd seen me and it had shocked him as much as his appearance had me.

"Maria?"

I shook the thoughts of William from my head and gave Tony my attention. "I won't forget you, Tony, no matter where I am. Yes, I'd love to go dancing. I haven't done that in a very long time."

The last time I'd danced, it had been with William. And later that night, we'd danced even more intimately, in the privacy of our cabin. My loins ached at the memory.

Tony beamed the whole way home.

Twenty Four

Tony kicked the truck tyre and swore. "Of all the times to get a flat tyre…"

"Of course," I responded. "It couldn't happen on a day when you don't have any deliveries, or even an hour earlier, when your cousins were still here. Do you want me to go pick up those motorcycle parts for you while you change the tyre?"

"Would you?" Tony asked eagerly. "If you

could just give the list to Armstrong and ask him about the cost, I can pick them up in the truck once it's going again. Then I might have my Indian fixed before you leave and I can take you for a ride along the Esplanade!"

I blushed. Tony had evidently seen me staring at his motorcycle and knew how much I wanted to fly on one. I plucked the list from inside the truck. "I'll take care of that now, then."

"Thank you." The clink of metal on metal ended in more swearing, so I hurried up the street toward Armstrong's Motor and Cycle Shop.

I pushed the door open and was greeted by a similar scene, though the disassembled Triumph was smaller than Tony's truck and the swearing was mostly in English, unlike Tony's vivid Italian.

"Good afternoon," I began.

A figure unfolded from behind the mess of muddy steel and stood up. "I'm sorry, miss, I didn't see you. Please pardon the language."

I laughed. "I hear worse than that at the fish market every day. One day, I'm going to tell them I understand Italian swear words." I looked closely at him and recognised the man who'd come second in yesterday's race. "OH! Congratulations on your near-win yesterday. You rode a very good race."

Mr Armstrong snorted. "Good enough to come second. The race wasn't all I lost yesterday. Lost a brand-new bike, too, unless I can fix it." He gestured at the mess.

"I thought you rode a Sun yesterday, not a Triumph." I stepped closer. "This wasn't your bike. The man who kept pace with Tony rode this one."

"My bike now, after it's taken a dip in the river. It might never go again. I wanted to compare it to the Sun and a friend of mine agreed to ride it in the race so we could see how she performed. He said if it was good enough for a half-day trial here, it'd survive the jungles where he lives. I ordered in two, 'specially. One for him and one for me. He even came down to Fremantle to test it out. He ships out tomorrow and this was supposed to be his. Instead, I had to give him mine – still in the crate it arrived in – and pray I can fix this one for myself."

I wanted William's bike with a lust I couldn't explain. I swore that if he rejected me, I'd return and buy myself a motorcycle with my savings. A throbbing engine between my legs far more powerful than any man. I remembered the paper in my hands. "Speaking of fixing motorcycles from yesterday's race, Tony Basile asked me to stop by and give you a list of the parts he needs. He said he could swing by later with his truck to pick them up."

Mr Armstrong nodded, wiped his muddy hands on his overalls, and reached for the list. "I don't know if we have all of these. Maybe at the Perth showroom. Might have to order some in. Better tell Basile…"

"You'll see him before I do," I said smoothly. "You tell him what you do and don't have when he turns up this afternoon. I'm going to a dance at the Hydrodome tonight and I can't go smelling of fish."

He laughed. "No, you can't. They'll think you're a mermaid who's traded her tail for legs for a night of revelry. And we all know how that story ends."

I summoned a smile that I didn't feel. "No, I'm not sure that I do, Mr Armstrong."

He opened his mouth to say something, but the shop door flew open and William marched in. My heart leaped as my mouth grew dry.

"Armstrong! I hope you don't think I'm taking that to the jungle with me in pieces. It'll be full of crabs in an hour — less if the bloody things are migrating. I need it on the wharf before dark in one piece."

"You took her for a swim, McGregor. I had to get a truck to pull her out — a foot deep in mud, she was. It'll take me a week to clean her out." He held up his hands in supplication. "But I liked the model so much I ordered myself one, too. Should be on the wharf, if the lumpers haven't loaded it aboard already. I'll keep this one instead. Not like I'll want to ride it in a hurry – my Sun beat you easily."

William nodded, his lips forming a fleeting smile before it was gone. "Fair enough. Thank you." He turned on his heel and walked out. For a moment, our eyes met and my lips formed his name, but no sound came out. His gaze slid over me as if I didn't exist and he didn't slow his step in the slightest.

The door banged behind him as I felt a hot tear trickle down my cheek. He'd seen me and deliberately ignored me. Why?

"That was rude, but you'll have to excuse McGregor. He works at a rough mining colony near Ceylon. A craggy rock called Christmas Island. No place for politeness there."

Numbly, I nodded, swivelling to face Mr Armstrong. I had to clear my throat twice before my voice returned. "What were you saying before about…about mermaids? And how their stories end?"

Mr Armstrong grinned. "It's an old fairy tale, miss. A mermaid who wanted a soul had to find a man to love her. He did, but he found someone better. She danced all night upon knives and the only way she could save herself was to kill her beloved. Instead, she threw herself into the waves and drowned." He shook his head. "Sad story. All mermaid stories are. Unhappy creatures, neither fish nor woman. Halfway between two worlds and part of neither."

A mermaid taking her own life instead of the unfaithful man? There was a fanciful tale indeed. No real mermaid would be so forgiving. I bade him good day and set off home. I had a dance to prepare for.

Twenty Five

"What do you have around your neck?" I stared at the black bow peeping out of Tony's starched collar. "Shouldn't you be wearing a tie?"

He straightened it nervously. "It is a tie – a bow tie. Mum said I should dress up properly and you…you look beautiful."

I blushed. It wasn't a word I'd heard often to describe me.

"Where did you get that necklace? The beads are pretty."

I gulped. I'd asked Charles to set a string of pale blue pearls for me and he'd done a beautiful job. This was the first occasion where I'd worn the pearl choker – or any necklace at all – and I kept reaching up to touch the strange thing at my throat. I managed to smile and avoid answering by focussing on fastening my shoes.

I called goodbye to Merry and she croaked out, "Enjoy yourself." It sounded like she started to say something else, but a coughing fit kept her from saying more. I promised I'd do as she said. Quietly, I closed the door behind me and followed Tony out to the street.

"Where's your truck?" I asked.

He grinned. "I thought we'd take the tram tonight. From your door to South Beach, without making you climb into truck cabs or soil that pretty blue skirt in the dust kicked up by my motorcycle." A pause. "Thank you for going to get those parts for me. I think some have to come by ship, so I'll be waiting a while. When you come back from visiting your mother, I'll have to take you for a ride."

"Sure," I replied. If and when I returned, I'd have my own motorcycle and we could go for a ride together.

We boarded the tram, Tony paid our fares, and he followed me to one of the few remaining seats. It looked like there were a lot of people headed to the Hydrodome tonight – and Tony wasn't the only one wearing a bow tie.

The end of the line was South Beach, just outside the huge, open, two-storey building that was the Hydrodome. The crush of people spilled out and we made for the tearooms, as Tony wanted to treat me to dinner. Tony ordered something with chicken, but I insisted on the fish because I knew we'd sold her fresh fillets that very morning.

"You spend every day working with fish – don't you grow tired of eating it? I know if I never saw another fish again, I wouldn't miss it." He laughed.

I tried to smile. "I don't know how long it will be until I eat fresh fish again. The food on the ship might not be very fresh at all. To me, this will always be the taste of home." I carefully forked a morsel into my mouth. Dhufish, I was certain.

His chicken arrived and food monopolised our mouths for some time. The sun slowly set over the ocean as I heard the faint sounds of the band tuning their instruments in the dance hall upstairs. Soon it would be time to dance.

Twenty Six

The jazz crept into my ears, my feet, my blood and very bones. My body moved to the music as if of its own accord. I danced through air instead of water, but it felt just as effortless.

"I should have taken you dancing sooner, if I knew you were so good on your feet," Tony said. Admiration shone through his eyes, but he wasn't the only one. Other men stared, too, to the irritation of their dance partners.

The song ended and the singer announced, "Our next one is an old favourite for all of you who are missing someone, or you know you're going to, when you say good night." The band launched into the opening bars and he started singing. "Come on, sing along. I know you all know the words."

I stumbled at the first line of *There is Somebody Waiting for Me*. This was the song I'd accidentally started singing along to on the *Trevessa*, with disastrous results that still made my skin crawl.

No. Some stories do end well for mermaids and we're not stupid enough to dance on knives for men who don't value us.

I excused myself, telling Tony I needed some air, and slipped outside. The moment my shoes hit the sand, I kicked them off and scooped them up. Not dancing on knives, but near enough. The sand between my toes was soothing and the moonlight caressing the water called to me. I wanted to step right into the water, dress and all, but there were too many people about. I sighed and stepped onto the jetty boardwalk surrounding the swimming baths which held up the shark-proof netting. My bare feet padded softly on the boards, a soothing rhythm that made me want to sing even more. How could I stay silent with such music in my heart?

I reached the end of the boardwalk, where it turned abruptly to fence off the deep end of the baths. I held tight to a light post and breathed deeply. More than ever, I wanted to step off into the water.

Heavy footsteps sounded on the boards behind me and I turned, expecting to see Tony. No. This man was broader across the shoulders and taller. He hunched over, shadowing his hanging head as if he wanted to escape the music as much as I did.

"That bloody song," he muttered.

My heart flew. "William," I breathed.

He stopped, perhaps six feet from me, and leaned against another light post. He pulled something out of his pocket, unscrewed the top, then held the flask to his lips. Three sizeable gulps later, he returned the bottle to its hiding place in his jacket.

I debated what to say. Should I simply greet him and ask if he enjoyed the music, making small talk like humans do? Or should I confront him, asking him why he'd been so rude in the motorcycle shop today?

William stole my thunder and spoke first. "I should have dived in after you. Never mind the sharks or the storm. I should have fought the men who held me back and jumped out of that damn lifeboat to help you. Better than living as a coward." He spat in the ocean. "You might have accepted me then, but not the man I am now. My heart died that day and I wish I'd died with it."

Tears sprang to my eyes and I couldn't speak. The heartbreak in his tone hammered every word home — another nail through my chest, deep into my heart. I heard the boards shift under his shoes as he walked away. Blindly, I tried to follow him, but my foot met only air and I splashed into the water instead.

Swearing, I dropped like a stone as my layers of clothing drank the salty water. Undeterred, I waded along the seabed to the shallows.

"Oh my God, Maria! Are you all right?" Tony raced into the water to help me, as if he hadn't seen me dive into the fishing boat harbour on more than one occasion.

"I'm fine," I said, embarrassed by the number of people on the beach, staring. "I slipped, is all."

Tony draped his jacket around my shoulders and steered me through the gawkers. Somehow, he acquired a towel that he passed me to me. I patted my skirt with it, but it became soaked before I was anywhere near dry. I looked around for William, but he was nowhere to be found. In the time it had taken me to walk ashore, he'd disappeared.

Sighing heavily, I let Tony take me back to the tram and home. Maybe mermaids shouldn't dance.

Twenty Seven

"Thank you for a lovely evening, Tony," I said as I reached Merry's veranda.

He followed me up the steps slowly. "I should have come out for air with you. Instead, I went to get you a drink and when I got outside, I couldn't find you anywhere. Anything could have happened to you when you slipped – you might have drowned! I'd never have forgiven myself if you'd been hurt."

I shrugged. "Maybe I should have stayed inside and danced longer. I'm fine. Really. Now tonight's even more unforgettable."

We both laughed as companionably as we did at work.

"Your ship leaves tomorrow, doesn't it?" he asked and I nodded. Both the next steamer for Southampton and the *Islander* left tomorrow. "So this is goodbye."

I didn't want to admit it. He was my friend, as dear to me as Merry. But I might never see him again.

"Maria. If I begged you to stay with me, I mean, STAY with me, now and always, would you not go? Would you marry me, Maria?"

Once the words were out, he couldn't unsay them. They hung in the air like the rail bridge had before it had crashed into the river and swirled out to sea. The one that had nearly killed us both.

"Tony…"

My friend silenced me. "Wait. Don't answer that. This is the wrong time to ask you. You have to go. I know that. You need to see your mother and it's not fair to ask you to choose between me and your family. Family is important. But please…don't forget me. There's a home here for you with me if you want it. Answer me when you come home. When you're ready." He took a deep, shaky breath. "I want to ask something else. Something I need you to answer." I waited. "May I kiss you goodbye?"

He stepped closer, advancing slowly as if I were a small creature he didn't want to frighten away. I fought down my tears and forced myself to answer, "Yes."

Tony's hands shook as he reached to cup my face. I stood still, unsure how to proceed, and let my friend guide our first kiss.

He smelled of peppermint – he'd been sucking the things since dinner. Now I knew why.

Tony pursed his lips and pressed them to mine in a gentle, chaste kiss that warmed my heart. But no more. After that brief contact, he pulled away.

"Good night. Safe voyage and may God bring you safe home again."

"Good night," I called after his retreating back, wishing I knew where home truly was.

Twenty Eight

"Do you have everything?" Merry asked, eyeing my steamer trunk. Even with my hat, gloves, shoes and coat draped across the top, the huge thing was still visible. I wasn't looking forward to dragging it down to the harbour.

I nodded. I'd packed and repacked the trunk so many times, I couldn't remember what had stayed and what would come with me. The exception was the books in the bottom. I'd packed the book Captain Foster wrote and my own, handwritten notebooks. I'd painstakingly recorded my memories of every conversation with William, in the hope that it would help me find him. Now that I understood the words, I realised just how much he'd said. How much I wished I'd been able to answer him.

A cup of tea clinked to the table in front of me. "Are you certain this is what you want?" Merry's grey eyes were filled with concern.

I took a deep breath. "Yes." My eyes filled with tears, threatening to spill over.

"What about Tony?"

"Tony wants me to stay. He wants me to stay so much he asked me to marry him last night." Merry opened her mouth to comment, so I continued, "But he said he didn't want an answer now. He wants me to tell him when I return."

"Will you?"

"Will I what?"

Merry sighed and sat at the table, across

from me. "Will you return, and will you accept his offer? He's been sweet on you for years. Surely you've seen it."

I bowed my head. I had, but many other men looked at me the same way. I'd long since learned that it was the nature of a siren to attract men like I did. "I don't know if I'll return, Aunt Merry. William has my heart…and I believe I hold his, too. I need to set things to rest with William before I can answer anything more about my future — including where and who I spend it with. I must go." I didn't want to meet her eyes. My tears would spill over if she so much as mentioned Tony's name again. He was a good man who didn't deserve a siren. He deserved a woman who would stand by his side through all things, which I could never promise to do.

"You must follow your heart," Merry said softly. "If it leads you far from here, I wish you every happiness, and if it leads you back here, you will always find a home in this house." I looked up in surprise. "Perhaps one day you will even bring children here. Now, don't discount the idea — you may find a man you wish to make your husband and children seem to come naturally when you have a husband in the house." She winked and I couldn't help but laugh.

"Merry, the chance of me ever settling down with a husband and children…"

She smiled. "The future holds many things for you, I'm sure, and happiness, too." She picked up her cup and drank the dregs of her tea. The last rays of afternoon sun slanted through the window, glinting on the gold edging on her cup.

Time to go.

Our eyes met and we both knew it was time. We rose and I rounded the table to her side. I'd never touched her and somehow I felt the occasion demanded it, yet I didn't know how.

Merry came to my rescue, as she had on the *Trevean*. Her frail-looking arms wrapped firmly around me, with more strength than I'd believed possible. She tilted her head up and kissed my cheek. "It has been a pleasure and a privilege to help you. You've been like a daughter to me, though I have no children. Take care, Maria Stella Maris, Maria Speranza…and any name you choose to take in the future."

"Thank you. Thank you…for everything you've done for me, Merry." I didn't feel like my words were anywhere near enough to convey my gratitude, but they made Merry smile.

I stepped into my shoes, pulled on my coat, and slid my hat down over my hair. Lastly, I slipped on my gloves. I grasped the steamer trunk's handle and heaved. And swore.

Merry laughed and followed me out as I lugged the stupid thing out to the veranda for the longest walk of my life. I was panting by the time I'd managed to get it to the street outside, and I turned to wave to Merry so I could catch my breath. A hundred yards down the road, I did the same – and again, until, on my third stop, I couldn't see her any more.

Grimly, I hauled my luggage to the bottom of the hill and sat on it for a rest. From here, though, I could see the *Islander* – and it looked like she was loading up to leave. With the ship in sight, I gritted my teeth and lifted the case, staggering to the wharf.

"I'll take that for you, miss. You travelling on the *Islander*?" The deep voice behind me made me jump, but I allowed the smiling lumper to take my trunk to the ship.

I straightened my hat, smoothed my skirt and fought to regain my breath. William might be aboard already and if I saw him, I'd need all the composure I could muster. I approached the vessel with my head held high. The captain was on deck, supervising the loading of the ship.

"Pardon me," I began, "but you said to return when you were about to leave, and it appears to be the case. Now can you tell me how much my passage will cost to Christmas Island?"

The captain stared at me for a moment, as if

he had no idea who I was. "We don't have space for so much as a kitten aboard, miss. That damn engineer's gone and bought half of Fremantle to take with him and a train to lug it up to Drumsite, or so he says. He's got cargo in all the cabins as well as the hold – his own cabin's so full he's bunking with the crew. If this won't be a voyage from hell, I don't know what will. Miss, best wait for the next run. We'll be back here in a few months. It's cyclone season, now, too, so it'll be a rough trip. Pity he doesn't get seasick."

I closed my gaping mouth with a snap. No space for me? I couldn't wait months. William was aboard this ship and I had to go with him. "Captain, you don't understand. I must travel on this ship. I can't wait. I must…"

The man shrugged. "There's nothing I can do, miss. Ask His Mightiness yourself. Maybe he'll give you a different answer – perhaps he'll agree to leave some of his precious cargo here to free up a cabin for you." He jerked his thumb at a figure striding along the wharf.

No, William wasn't aboard the ship. But he soon would be.

I watched him walk across the gangplank and cross the deck. I felt like I was in the motorcycle shop all over again. "Make sure everything's aboard, Captain Hughes. Even if we have to lash some of the crates to the deck. I'll be below in my cabin." He strode past me as if I didn't exist, and disappeared down a hatch.

The captain cleared his throat. "I'm sorry, miss. You heard him. Maybe next time." He walked away.

I clenched my fists at my sides. I had the money to pay for my passage – ten times over, I was certain of it – and yet he refused to take it. I stormed off the ship.

I could go home. I could wait. I could ask for someone to fetch my things from the hold and return to Merry. I could tell her I'd changed my mind and that I wanted to stay with her. And Tony…

No. My anger blazed and the entire Indian

Ocean couldn't quench this fire. No ship captain or engineer denied the ocean's gift passage on her ocean.

I rounded the remaining crates placed on the edge of the wharf and peered into the water. The light was fading fast. If I slipped into the water and approached the boat from the harbour side…she was sitting so low in the water, I could grasp the ladder or one of the ropes on that side with little trouble. All I had to do was make it over the rail and slip into the hold.

I sat on the edge, dangling my legs over the dark water, then lowered myself in. I kicked my shoes off as I felt my hat float away, but I didn't care any more. I had clothes in my trunk – I just needed to reach it. Ducking under a wave, I swam around the stern. I bobbed gently in the waves, looking for a suitable place to climb up. Ha – there were steps cut into the side of the ship as if people frequently needed to go from a ship to a launch.

Trying to be quiet, I crept up the stairs and

hid just below the railing, listening for anyone nearby. When I was satisfied that I was alone, I rose and hurried into the shadows before anyone could come to discover me. No one noticed me as I watched two crewmen carry crates into what looked like a cabin, already filled with wooden boxes stacked as high as the top bunk. A third man walked past at a much slower pace, lugging my trunk. This went through a hatch at the end of the passage that I presumed led to the hold. He returned a minute later without my luggage, heading back to the main deck.

Quickly, I sneaked into the full cabin and dragged the blankets off the two top bunks, then seized the pillows, too. Bundling the lot into my arms, I carried it through the dark hatch and into the cargo hold.

I scanned the stacked crates and found what I wanted – one slightly lower than the stacks on either side, yet large enough for me to stretch out on top of it, hidden from sight. I spread my blankets out across what I intended to be my bunk and left the pillows in the hidey-hole. I wanted to change into dry clothes, but I felt it best to hide until the ship was underway. That way, if they caught me, at least I couldn't be put ashore before Christmas Island.

So I sat, huddled in a blanket, and waited for the boilers to fire up. The clunk of the tug hooking on to the ship took me by surprise, until I remembered that this was normal for Gage Roads. The firemen would stoke the boilers while the tug towed her out of the harbour. Once in the shipping channel, the vessel's engines would kick in and she'd move under her own power.

More clunking against the hull echoed through the hold as the tug disengaged. Now all I could hear was the engines' hum and the swish of water against the hull.

Time to start a new adventure. After I'd made William answer for his rudeness and the cryptic comments he'd made last night. I might pretend to be human, but I was one of the true daughters of the ocean's gift. And my trials had barely begun.

Twenty Nine

This could be the craziest thing I've done yet. At least this boat had an engine and I was wearing clothes. If only they weren't damp and full of salt.

I cursed quietly, but the sound echoed through the hold. I'd meant to change them as soon as the ship was properly under way, but it seemed that the hum of the engines had lulled me to sleep. I climbed out of my blanket-lined burrow amid the crates and stiffly made my way to my trunk. What I'd give for a proper mattress to sleep on. Perhaps I'd borrow one from one of the unoccupied cabins – ugh, or maybe more than one. I'd grown soft in my time on land.

Stripping off my soiled clothes, I wished for a washroom – or a wash basin – or…at this point, I'd take a bucket of fresh seawater. Hang on. The passenger cabins I'd seen had wash basins. They'd been hidden behind crates of cargo, but they'd been there. All I had to do was sneak into one and I could get clean.

I grabbed a clean dress from my trunk and padded across to the hatch. I held my breath and listened, but I heard no one near. I crept along the passage and slipped into the first cabin. Clambering over the crates to the sink was a challenge, but there was a small gap between the wall and the cargo that was just large enough to conceal me – while I had full use of the washbasin.

I turned the tap on and cupped water in my

hands, drinking deeply before splashing some on my face and chest. I hadn't thought to bring a flannel or a towel, so I washed myself as best I could before drying myself with a sheet from the bunk. I debated whether to rinse my clothes or just let them finish drying, seeing as they were close to it already, when I heard male voices. I dropped to a crouch and tried to shrink further behind the crates.

"I tell you, I saw a woman walk along the passage and into this cabin," one man insisted.

"There aren't any passengers on this side. The cabins are all full of supplies Grumpy McGregor ordered in Fremantle. There's definitely no women aboard," the second man scoffed.

The voices sounded like they were just outside the door. The wide open door, I realised, wishing I'd thought to close it behind me. "I know what I saw. She had tits as big as melons. Not one of them flappers – a real woman."

Melons? I glanced down, horrified at the

thought that I was carrying around melons. My breasts were nowhere near that big.

"Melons?" the second man echoed. "Next thing you'll tell me she was beautiful, too, and beckoning." His pitch crept impossibly high. "Come to my cabin, Black, and I'll show you my melons."

Black laughed. "Didn't need to go into the cabin to see 'em. She was as naked as the day she was born. I could see every jiggle as she walked…"

"You're daft. Not three hours out of port and you're imagining naked women with enormous tits. Next thing, you'll be seeing mermaids."

Both men laughed and their voices faded away.

I slowly let out the breath I hadn't realised I'd been holding. As if either or even both of the men together had posed a danger to me. I laughed silently as I pulled my clean dress over my head.

I was on a ship with William, headed to

Christmas Island. One way or another, I intended to reclaim my heart. Just as long as they didn't kick me off the boat. That's what happened to stowaways.

Thirty

I waited for what felt like an interminable time before I dared move. I definitely didn't want the men seeing mermaids – especially not this one. Pulling a blanket off the nearest bunk, I shrouded myself in it, so that the grey wool covered my fair hair and skin, and most of my blue dress, too. Hopefully, this would hide me from distant eyes as I prowled the ship. This vessel had electric lighting just like the

Trevessa had had – much too bright to hide in.

I clung to the shadows as I crept along the passage. All the closely-spaced doors seemed to open into cabins the same as the first one, so I didn't waste time with them. I needed to find food, my grumbling stomach told me. I climbed a ladder to the deck above and continued my search.

The sound of snoring emanated from the open door at the aft end of the passage, drawing me closer. Was this where the crew cabins were…and with them, William? Eagerly, I peeped into the room. Four bunks each held a blanketed body. The snoring came from the top bunk which had a slim, brown arm hanging down from it. Whoever he was, he wasn't William. I scanned the bunk below him, then the two on the other side. There wasn't much to see until movement made me look closer. The light outside glittered off a pair of open eyes in the lower bunk.

My heart stuttered as William's eyes bored into mine. I couldn't speak for fear of breaking the connection, but I had so much I wanted to say. So much to tell and even more questions to ask. I wanted…

He grunted and rolled onto his side, facing the bulkhead.

I almost cried. I took a step into the cabin, reaching for William so I could pull him back to where he could see me so we could talk, before reason returned and I realised that was a stupid idea. If the others woke up, I'd be in a lot of trouble, and I might not have enough time to explain to William why I was aboard the ship before they interrupted.

Reluctantly, I forced myself to leave. Tears spilled down my face, blurring my vision, so I stumbled through the nearest open hatch instead of crying in the corridor. This room was bigger than the cabins – I managed to walk several paces before my hip bumped painfully into a table. Blinking, I looked around at the ship's mess hall. If I'd believed in Merry's religion, I might have thanked the deity in charge, but I contented myself with a smile of victory as I strode to the door that I was certain led to the galley and, hopefully, some food.

The darkened kitchen was much larger than Merry's, but I couldn't see the icebox anywhere. The low-ceilinged room was full of benches and utensils, but there was no food in sight. Incensed, I scanned the room, looking for the large pantry that must be required to feed the whole crew for the voyage. I spotted a door partially concealed behind a shelving unit full of crockery and that's where I headed next.

In the light spilling through the bank of open windows, I saw that this room was full of humming iceboxes. Perhaps these were the new refrigerators I'd seen advertised in the newspaper. If they were, then they held my next meal.

I yanked on the lever and opened it. I almost moaned as I saw a bottle of milk in front, the cream already rising to the top.

Someone will miss it, I told myself as I lifted the bottle off the shelf, revealing a row of more behind it.

I didn't care.

I drank deeply from the lip of the bottle, knowing Merry would frown and shake her head if she saw me, but I didn't dare go and find something more civilised to drink from. The liquid calmed the snarling in my stomach and I finished off what must have been almost a quart of milk, but it tasted so good.

Levering open the next icebox or refrigerator or...whatever it was, I became transfixed by a familiar Mills and Wares tin. Why keep biscuits in the icebox? Unless the tin held something more perishable than biscuits. Holding my breath in anticipation, I pulled the tin from the shelf and cracked the lid. I smelled chocolate before I saw the half-eaten cake, but my mouth was watering too much to let me return the delicacy to the shelf without tasting it. Cake required cutlery, though — at least to cut it. I carried my prize to the galley and found a suitable knife. The blade scraped against the bottom of the tin as I cut myself a generous slice.

The first bite was heavenly – no one made a cake like Mills and Wares. I lifted the piece to my mouth to take another and heard shuffling footsteps in the mess hall. I fled to the refrigerator room. Just in time, I realised as the galley light clicked on. I hid behind the furthest refrigerator from the door, sinking onto the floor in the hope that whoever it was wouldn't see me.

"Bloody McGregor. If he leaves his sweets about like this, the rats will get them and serve him right. Not like he shares any with the rest of us. Probably counts every crumb, too."

I held my breath as the shuffling steps approached my hiding spot. I heard the sound of a refrigerator door opening, then the clink of the tin on the metal shelf, and the door closed again. I breathed again when I heard clanking in the kitchen.

"Tea for the officer on watch…damn, but I haven't missed night duties while we were in port. Haven't missed McGregor, neither…"

The cook continued to mutter as he made tea. It seemed like an eternity before he left with his rattling tray, turning the lights off on his way out.

I'd finished my cake as quietly as I could. William's cake, I supposed, but he'd been a right arse to me, not letting me pay my passage like a normal passenger. It was because of him that I was forced to scavenge for food instead of enjoying my meals in the mess like everyone else. I marched back to the refrigerator that held the cake and tucked the tin under my arm. I grabbed another bottle of milk, too.

Hoping this would tide me over until breakfast, I sneaked back to the hold and my hidey-hole. Let William wonder what had happened to his chocolate cake as he slept.

Thirty One

I woke up thirsty, wishing I hadn't finished up all the milk last night. A quick, cautious peek outside told me I'd slept until the early afternoon, judging by the slight westerly angle of the sun. Mindful of last night's near-discovery. I returned to the hold to hide until darkness fell.

Easier said than done.

For an hour, I tried not to think about how much I wanted a glass of cool, clear water. In desperation, I dug out Captain Foster's book about their journey in the *Trevessa*'s lifeboats, wondering how they dealt with thirst. The book was distinctly unhelpful – the men sucked buttons, bathed in seawater and caught rainwater in anything they could, none of which seemed particularly practical advice. There was neither seawater nor rain in this hold and I had no intention of sucking at the buttons on my dress.

Angrily, I stalked the hold, examining the crates and boxes for something to quench my thirst. Flour, rice, sugar, cooking oil, toilet paper…my mouth seemed to grow drier still as I read the letters stamped on the cargo. I let out a whoop when I discovered one marked MILK, but fifteen minutes with a crowbar left me swearing. The crate did contain milk – row upon row of tinned, condensed milk. The sickly sweet stuff that I'd gagged on in the lifeboat. If I'd had a tin opener, I might have cracked one open anyway, but the best tool I had was the crowbar. Surely I could find something better. If not...I swallowed with difficulty, knowing I'd choke it down if I had to.

I checked every crate I could reach or read, but most seemed to be heavy machinery. The rest of the food stores must be in the boxes in the cabins I hadn't been allowed to sleep in, I decided. Of course they would be. Right beside the nearest drinking water that I couldn't reach 'til dark.

Annoyed, I flopped onto my makeshift bed. If it had to be the gooey milk, then so be it. I glanced at the crate that obscured my hidey-hole from the entrance to the hold and traced the letters: Roma Fruit Palace.

My hopes rose, but I squashed them quickly. Roma stocked plenty of things and it seemed more likely that this was full of tins or other bulk supplies than something as perishable as fruit.

Yet the crate was directly below one of the loading hatches – it might have been one of the last things winched aboard. So maybe...

Sighing, I hopped down and retrieved my crowbar. Five minutes later, I squealed in excitement at the watermelons in the crate. I was in heaven.

I hefted the smallest one I could reach — easily twenty pounds of fruit — and dropped it onto the deck. It smashed in a satisfying splatter of coral-coloured flesh. I slid down to claim my spoils.

Armed with a knife I'd borrowed to cut the cake, I carved chunks out of the lopsided bowl of melon rind that sat between my crossed legs. The sweet melon melted on my tongue, making me moan with longing for more. I caught myself before I made too much noise — I didn't want the *Islander*'s crew to catch me because of a melon. Even as I forced myself to enjoy my meal in silence, I'd never derived so much pleasure from fruit before.

A trickle of juice squirted down the front of my dress, oozing between my breasts. A sudden image of William licking the sweetness from my bare breasts left me with longing for the real thing. Just the feeling of his hands on my body and his lips and tongue on my skin…

What was wrong with me? I felt unusually warm and all I could think of was William. Yes, I wanted to kick him or knock him to the ground for his rudeness. But then I wanted us to shed our clothes and indulge this raging lust that inflamed my mind. All night.

I smothered the laughter that threatened to bubble up. For the whole time I'd lived with Merry, I'd managed to control myself and now I was ready to jump William at the slightest hint he was still interested. So much for being the sedate young lady Merry had tried to turn me into in Fremantle. I needed air, I decided. The cool, stiff, night breeze off the ocean as we steamed north to the tropical island William now called home.

I busied myself with cleaning up as much of the smashed watermelon as I could – putting the salvageable pieces back in the crate for later and resolving to clean the sticky mess on the floor as soon as I could lay my hands on a bucket and mop.

Somewhere above me, a dinner bell rang. That meant evening and, hopefully, darkness. I grabbed my empty milk bottle and hurried to the hatch.

No one seemed to be around, but I'd been wrong before, so I donned a blanket again to creep up to the nearest unoccupied cabin. I rinsed out the milk residue and filled the bottle with water. I drank it down, barely pausing for breath, before filling it up again. I screwed the cap back on, intending to take it back to the hold with me, but the stickiness of my fingers made me want to wash more thoroughly. I washed my hands and then my forearms, lifting my feet one at a time to wash from my toes to my knees, which was as high as I could reach without stripping off entirely. A proper wash could wait until later, when there was no one about.

The running water had awoken another need that became increasingly urgent. I crept along the passage to the nearest head and made use of the facilities. Whatever man had used it last hadn't seen fit to flush it, so I pulled the chain without thinking. The roar of the plumbing could surely be heard halfway across the ship, so I did my business in record time, flushed again and scurried out as quickly as I could. I raced back to the cabin for my bottle of water and I'd made it halfway back to the hold before I stopped dead at the sound of voices.

"Captain said to make sure none of the pipes up here are leaking. With everyone at dinner, there's no reason for water to be running here, so there must be a leak. More'n likely, someone just left the tap on or the washer's gone, but we don't want to run out of drinking water from a leak. McGregor'd probably make us drink our own piss like shipwrecked sailors instead of putting in at the nearest port for more water. He says he was shipwrecked once — three weeks at sea in a little lifeboat with twenty other men, poor bastards. It's a wonder they didn't throw him overboard when they had a chance and save the world a lot of misery."

A different voice sniggered. "D'you think that's what made him so sour? Drinking his own piss?"

"Dunno. I think he was born that way. Not even his mother could love such a mean bastard. Can you imagine him smiling?"

"I heard he smiled at one of the girls in the White House on the island and she fainted in shock."

"Before or after?"

"Probably after she was done servicing him. Why would he smile before?"

A pause before the first voice finally said, "I could do with a turn with one of those White House girls. The ones in Fremantle cost too much. I could spend a whole night with Su or Lian in the White House for the price those Australian girls wanted for ten minutes!"

Another pause. "But what d'you need with more than ten minutes?"

"You barely get your wick wet with ten

minutes. I want a good hour, at least. First a quick poke while she squeals, then get her down on her knees to get me ready again so I can take my time the second time around. You haven't had a woman properly unless she's walking bow-legged the next day as if she can still feel you inside her."

What I'd give for ten minutes more with William. Or an hour…but better to have a whole night. That's all we'd ever had together and I wanted another night more than I could say. The hard heat of him between my legs, driving us both to the peak of pleasure…

The bottle I'd been stroking in a cold imitation of what I really wanted slipped from my fingers and landed heavily on my foot. Smothering my yelp, I watched it roll toward the edge of the deck. If it fell, it would hit the deck below and alert the men to my presence.

I'd seen what happened when lust-crazed crewmen looked at me on a lonely voyage. It would end in me killing them, like it had last time.

I dived and grabbed it, just before it reached the edge. I heard the clatter of shoes on the ladder at the end of the passage, so I jumped to my feet, tucked the bottle under my arm, and swung over the railing to the level below. I sprinted for the hold and made it into the darkness before I dared to breathe again. Sinking to the deck, panting, I swore I'd stay hidden until everyone was asleep. At least I now had water.

Thirty Two

My stomach was roaring like some sort of sea monster by the time I felt it was late enough to venture out. This time, I headed straight for the galley. I wanted more than milk and cake, and I wanted a tin opener, too.

In the refrigerator room, I found a door that led to a larder full of tins, boxes and sacks. Seizing a near-empty flour sack, I started stuffing tins into it, grateful that the flour dregs muffled the clanking. When the sack's stitching started to look strained, I grabbed a dented, metal bucket and started filling that, too.

I set my bucket and bag of supplies down next to a mop and advanced on the refrigerators. The canned supplies were for later, but I wanted something I could wolf down now. Smearing butter and some sort of jam on a hastily carved slab of bread, I sank my teeth through the crust. Crunchy and starting to go stale, the bread was the best I'd ever tasted. Silently, I apologised to Merry and all the fine bakers in Fremantle, but I'd never been so hungry before. On a ship this fast, I couldn't even catch fish to sustain me. Mermaids were never made to sail in steamships, I decided as I resolved not to travel in them in future. When my business with William was over, then I would swim home. Sooner, rather than later, I hoped.

Most of the food in the refrigerators was raw and waiting to be cooked, but I didn't dare take the time to cook myself a meal. A more than proficient cook, thanks to Merry's painstaking lessons in the kitchen, I still didn't enjoy the activity much. Maybe if I had a man I loved to cook for…Sal's words in the fruit shop came back to me and I felt my face grow hot. I had more enthusiasm for heating things up in the bedroom than the kitchen. Or a ship's cabin, I thought, remembering the one blissful night William and I had spent together in his cabin on the *Trevessa*. I could revisit the cabin on the sea floor as many times as I wished, but to get that time back was impossible. I might never spend another night with him – but I was determined to find out for sure.

But not before we reached his island.

Holding the remaining bread between my teeth, I carried my bucket, sack and mop back to the hold. I stacked the supplies in my hidey-hole and headed to the washroom to fill the bucket with water to deal with the melon mess.

I was already angry by the time I returned to the hold. In the process of climbing up and down ladders with a bucket, I'd managed to soak my skirt in soapy water. I dunked the mop in the bucket and was just about to pull it out when I heard chittering.

A rat sat in my bedding, nibbling on the remains of my bread while another relieved itself on the blanket before sniffing at my food.

I seized the mop and cracked the handle across the crate. Two dead rats lay on either side of a slice of bread with a mop-handle-shaped dent across it. I wiped the jam off the handle with my fingers and rinsed them in the bucket. Swearing, I quickly sloshed the water across the floor, then grabbed the rats, soiled blanket and bread and stuffed them into the empty bucket. Trying to keep the anger out of my tone, I sat down and sang, summoning any creature within earshot to me. I might have to sleep in the hold, but I didn't have to share it with vermin.

Rats appeared from everywhere. Five…a dozen, then thirty or more. All assembled in the puddle on my freshly-mopped floor. I stood up and told them to follow me, swinging my bucket as I approached the rail on the aft deck. I tipped my bucket over the railing and told the rats to follow it. In the darkness, a furry waterfall cascaded into the waves.

I set off to return the mop and bucket to the kitchen – and to replace my stolen slice of bread. The mulberry jam reminded me of Merry and I needed a little sweetness tonight to replace the bitterness that had settled in my heart.

I hadn't bargained on fighting the rats for food on this ship. What else would go wrong on this voyage? Or was my whole mission a mistake?

Thirty Three

I crammed the slice of bread into my mouth and strode toward the foredeck. I needed air and I needed to see the sky and feel the wind. I'd been cooped up in the hold for too long.

The night breeze caressed me as I stepped down the ladder, making me smile. I might not be able to fish from a ship moving this fast, but the ever-present wind from our passage was a refreshing compensation.

A high-pitched chitter stopped me in my tracks. *Not more rats!* I hurried toward the source of the sound, only to realise what I heard came from the water and it was too musical to be rats. Dolphins. Lots of them, by the sound of it.

I leaned over the side and caught sight of moonlight glinting on the slick bodies leaping in the ship's bow wave. I smiled and called a greeting, which they returned. I relaxed against the rail, happy to watch the dolphins play as I wished I could join them. Soon, perhaps.

"Storm and good fishing!" one of the dolphins remarked and a rill of agreement trickled through the pod.

Storm? Oh no – not this ship, too. I peered into the distance and saw where the stars ended. All along the horizon, clouds were massing for what looked like one hell of a tropical storm.

A scraping sound caught my attention and I realised there was another shadow silhouetted against the railing. William's broad shoulders were unmistakeable as he leaned over to look at the dolphins, just as I had. "Dolphins, not fish. She thought they were fish," I heard him murmur, before he laughed softly.

He was talking about me. I'd tried to tell him that the dolphins surfing the *Trevessa*'s bow wave were hunting flying fish, but I hadn't known the words to explain. Now he thought I was some sort of idiot, mistaking dolphins for fish as if I couldn't speak to them at will.

I opened my mouth to speak, but I deliberately stuffed the last of my mulberry-flavoured bread into it instead. William would report a stowaway just as surely as any other man on the ship, especially if he were as angry as he was I'd met on the day we left port. There was no sign of recognition or tenderness left in that man – Grumpy McGregor, the bane of the captain's existence, or so it seemed.

What had happened to the wonderful William who'd pulled me out of the ocean, helped me at every turn and fought for me with word and blow until the ship sank? The same man who'd lifted me tenderly into Captain Foster's lifeboat, telling me not to be afraid, for he'd keep me safe.

"What I'd give to have her here again. If I could have kept her safe," he whispered, as if he was reading my thoughts.

I stepped closer, desperate to touch him, to let him know I was here, watching the dolphins beside him.

William gave a huge sniff, wiping the salt spray from his face, before he turned and walked right past me as if he never saw me. Perhaps he didn't – for the salt seemed to have gotten into his eyes, irritating them to the point of tears.

Thirty Four

The waves crashing against the hull reminded me of being trapped in the cargo hold of the *Trevessa*, knowing that my only way out would sink the ship. But if this ship sank, I'd carry William to safety in my arms, if I had to, I swore to myself in the dark. Yet as the ship rolled in the mountainous seas, I couldn't rest. How could I sleep, knowing I might have to leap into action at any time and shift into my true form? Giuseppe's death had taught me that lesson and I'd never forget it. Nor would I let William drown while I drew breath.

I forced myself to stay in the hold as the storm's intensity increased. Open a tin and eat something, I urged myself. I crunched the tin opener through the nearest lid and almost gagged at the smell of old fish. I had to get this out of here before the smell permeated the hold, or it would stay with me for days. I bolted for the side, throwing the open can into the waves as they greedily licked up the side of the ship. Reason told me to go back to the hold, but I was too restless for that.

I needed to feel the storm, I decided. Nothing calmed me like the feeling of a power greater than myself, pushing and pulling on my body as if I had no control over it any more. The ocean…or the storm.

A gust of wind caught me as I reached the foredeck and I opened my arms to it, letting my concealing blanket fall to the deck. The air was so full of spray I could taste the salt on my lips. Home. The taste of home. I rushed to the bow, leaning out over the rail. A wave splashed high and I gasped as the water soaked me to the skin. I ached to dive in and swim with the storm. And once it was calm? I'd never catch up to the boat and William – perhaps I'd swim back to Fremantle. William didn't want me here. I stared down at the tempting water. Oh, so tempting…

"Don't!" a hoarse voice said. "I can't bear to watch it again. You leaping to your death away from me. As if being at sea in a storm wasn't already enough to give me nightmares."

I whirled around. William sat in the shadow of the bulkhead and I'd walked right past him.

"It was bad enough in the lifeboat, seeing you die every day and knowing it wasn't real. The other men told me I was mad, trying to jump into the ocean after a girl who wasn't there. They didn't understand I wasn't trying to save you – I just wanted to join you."

Tears welled up and I couldn't seem to close my mouth, so great was my horror. William had tried to kill himself – more than once.

"If I see you jump one more time, I swear I'll follow you, Maria. To the bottom of the bloody ocean or into the belly of a shark. I don't care any more. I should have known I wouldn't be the only one who couldn't sleep through a storm at sea. You'd be restless, too, and it was only a matter of time before you showed yourself."

He knew I was aboard the ship? After how carefully I'd hidden from everyone? "William, please, I…"

William waved me into silence. "Go back to wherever you hide when you're not tormenting me. Before one of the men on watch hears me talking to you and thinks I'm crazy. I know this ship's built to withstand tropical cyclones, but every storm we encounter takes away any hope I had of sleeping, just like on the *Trevessa*'s lifeboat. Maybe I am crazy, after all. Just not quite crazy enough to jump over the side yet."

I hesitated. This William was one I didn't know. The bitterness, the anger and the heart-wrenching despair weren't a part of the man I'd known and loved. Had he summoned all of these demons in his time in the lifeboat? I wanted to reach out to comfort him, as he'd done so many times for me, but I didn't dare. I was terrified he'd push me away.

"Good night," I whispered, feeling tears spill down my cheeks again as I trotted back to the darkness of the hold.

Thirty Five

I finished up the last tin of peaches as I felt the engines change their tune. We were slowing, presumably to make port. It wasn't completely dark outside yet, so I forced myself to stay hidden, hoping I'd find a chance to slip off the ship and into the water before I was discovered in the hold. If I was really lucky, they wouldn't unload 'til morning, but I couldn't count on that.

For the first time since we'd left Fremantle, the engines' hum sputtered and died. The silence was unnerving, or it would have been, if I couldn't still hear the swish of waves against the hull. Yet I didn't hear the impact of the hull against a jetty or pier, nor the sound of mooring ropes clinking against the ship. Not even the grind of the anchor being let down. I itched to see where we were and why we'd stopped.

The seconds ticked away like hours until I finally felt it was late enough to venture out without being seen. To my surprise, we weren't in port at all. The island rose out of the darkness as a hulking shadow to the north, off the port bow. The waves had died down somewhat, whispering against the hull as they glided past us, but I could hear the echoing boom as they pounded somewhere else. The other side of the island, perhaps, or the fringing reef. It was too dark to tell from the surface – I'd have to slip into the sea to investigate fully.

I heard voices and slipped into the shadows instead.

"Bloody Christmas Island. We get here a day early and the swell's running wrong. So we're off Waterfall, freezing our balls off, instead of balls-deep in one of the ladies at the White House in Flying Fish Cove."

"You don't have any balls to freeze off. Cap'n said the nor'westerly's slackening and the cove will be calm as a millpond in the morning. Maybe the ladies'll wake up early so you can dip your wick."

"Maybe I'll find your naked melon-girl hiding in my bunk and do her instead while I'm waiting."

"You'll need to get it up first…"

I shook my head at their frustrated banter. What woman would tolerate a man like that? They thought about nothing but sex, even when they weren't having any. In between the innuendo and insults, though, they'd told me that we were drifting in the lee of our destination, Christmas Island, and the port faced north-west. What I didn't know was how long a swim it would be to get there, but my clothes would only be a hindrance. Particularly after my enforced laziness of the last few weeks, as I couldn't swim and stay with the ship. I'd need to shake the stiffness out of my tail and what better way than a search for the port?

I crept back to the hold and stripped naked, folding my clothes into my trunk. I dragged it over beside William's, which I knew were his from reading their tags. I hoped mine would be landed alongside his and hopefully even taken to his house – though I didn't hold high hopes for this last. He'd surely know it wasn't his luggage, but if someone else delivered his things, I had a chance. As an afterthought, I pulled one of the tags from his case and fastened it around the handle of mine. There. That would ensure my belongings made it ashore.

As for me…I padded quietly to the foredeck and peered over the bow. My body tingled in anticipation at finally swimming again. Carefully, I climbed over the railing so there was nothing between me and the waves. I took a deep breath and dived.

Shouts came from the deck. "I saw her! I swear I saw the naked girl with the huge tits! She was right here!"

Laughing, I ducked under the surface and shivered at the thrill of shifting back to my true form. Tail, fins, flukes, gills…I gulped seawater and flooded my gills for the first time in weeks. Now all I wanted was some fresh fish and I'd feel like myself again. But first I had to find the port, I reminded myself.

I rippled my body, from top to tail, trying to work the kinks out of it after being cooped up in the hold for so long. Even my shoulders felt stiff. I rounded the north-east point and saw lights up on the cliff, so I swam faster toward them. I was met with an even higher cliff, so I kept going, skirting the rocks until they widened out into a sheltered cove. And it was sheltered, despite facing north-west – the swell had already died down. A narrow beach stretched across a section of the cove, which was ringed by precipitous cliffs everywhere else. Behind the beach and the houses terracing the slope above it, another cliff rose in the middle of the island, easily a hundred feet high again. A road wound its way up from the beach – heading toward the cliffs nearest the *Islander*'s sheltered bay.

I sang up a school of small fish – perhaps the length of my hand, perfect for swallowing whole – and selected several to satisfy my hunger. I snapped their necks quickly, but I didn't stop to eat yet.

Some houses still had lights on and I swam closer to investigate. The nearest stood on the cliffs by the pier – a white bungalow with few windows. On the veranda, I could see a woman and several men clustered around a table. They appeared to be playing some sort of game. It looked similar to what the Chinese grocers in Fremantle played late into the night, when their shops were shut. Unlike the grocers, though, these men were betting with tokens instead of money. The game finished and one man seemed to have won a large haul of tokens, but instead of seizing the pot, he grabbed the woman instead. None of the others seemed to find this strange. Instead, they sloped off into the building.

The couple stood alone on the veranda for a moment and the man said something I couldn't catch. Then the woman sank to her knees in front of him, so I could only see her head. The man dropped his pants to his ankles so his bits flopped out. To my surprise, the woman grabbed his dick and stuffed it into her mouth.

Intrigued, I lifted a fish and swallowed it, followed by a second. The woman seemed to be able to relax her throat, much as I did – she managed to get him down her throat, so that her chin rested against his balls. I wondered if the man tasted as good as my fish. Privately, I doubted it, though the woman didn't recoil in distaste. I watched her pull him in and out of her mouth a few times, as if he was trolling for fish in her throat, until the man lost control of himself and ejaculated fluid all over her face and front. She smiled and giggled as if this was perfectly acceptable, right up until the man left, when she angrily wiped herself with the hem of her tunic and hurried inside. I waited for some time before she reappeared in a dry tunic with another group of men in tow. The men sat down and started another game, gambling for the prize of this woman's time and attentions.

As I finished up my fish, I wondered at this oral sex act. The man had certainly seemed to enjoy it, but surely it didn't have to be so messy. If he'd managed to keep himself in her mouth or aimed for the floor instead of spraying her, or if she'd held onto him and perhaps swallowed his fluid…or wrapping him in a towel when he started spurting stuff everywhere…

It didn't seem difficult, I decided. Maybe I should try it on a man some day, if only to find out what he tasted like. I could always bite his bits off if I didn't like the experience.

The sound of an engine caught my attention – it was the *Islander*, slowly motoring into the cove as night faded into dawn. I slipped beneath the surface, still thinking about this strange form of sex.

Thirty Six

The coral surrounding this island was remarkable – the whole island was a drop-off, I found. I hid beneath the triangular jetty and watched William and the crew disembark. Just like the *Trevean*, they starting unloading the cargo as quickly as they could from the *Islander*. People onshore assisted with transport and distribution, before disappearing into the houses dotting the shoreline and the cliffs above.

Last to be winched ashore were some very large crates. William and another man seemed very excited by these.

"They say it's the biggest locomotive Peckett's ever built."

"I'll make arrangements to have it hauled up to the workshop tomorrow so we can assemble it."

"With the bigger firebox, we'll be able to speed up transport and shift double the volume in the same time…"

"It's the direct oil-burning engine that makes the difference. Not having to use wood any more."

"The startup time is far less than the Shays. Under an hour, they say."

"We'll be able to replace the old Shays with Pecketts in a matter of months."

I couldn't discern one voice from the other, for both men shared the burr in their speech that until now, I'd only heard in William's words.

"Wait until you see the other fine piece of engineering I brought home, Jackson."

I watched William pry open a crate that was somewhat smaller than the rest. He brushed the straw away to reveal a Triumph motorcycle, the twin to the one he'd ridden in the race back in Perth.

"The new P series. Beats your Trusty relic from the Great War – like comparing a Peckett to a Shay!"

Jackson whistled, admiring the machine as much as I did. "But can you ride it, McGregor? I seem to recall the last time I let you ride my Trusty, you took a spill and you were lucky we found you before you became a crab's dinner!"

"Find me some fuel and I'll race you to Rocky Point. Then we'll see who can handle a motorcycle."

The two men freed the Triumph from its crate and poured a liberal amount of liquid in its tank. William stomped on the kickstart lever by the back wheel a few times before the engine coughed into life, but his wide grin spoke volumes about his confidence.

Jackson wheeled up a less shiny motorcycle that looked like an older, more used version of William's. His took considerably longer to kick into life, but once the engine caught, it chugged like its younger counterpart. Both men nodded in unison three times before they took off, roaring up the road and the hill beyond until they were hidden from my sight.

I sighed. Seven years on land and I'd come full circle – I was naked in the water, wanting to join the human community, with no idea how to do it. And, once again, the human I wanted to join with most was William.

Thirty Seven

Until darkness fell once more, I explored the coral surrounding this island. It stuck up from the seabed like a sharp cone, though the point had been lopped off long since, leaving the cloud-shrouded plateau. I itched to climb it, to feel cloud on my skin and see where the huge frigate birds soared from, as they rode the thermals down to the sea. Around the edges, the coastline of the island was full of cliffs, caves and tiny coves, the biggest of which was Flying Fish Cove, where the *Islander* and the jetty were.

I was lucky; the moon hadn't yet risen when I stepped out of the ocean and onto the strip of beach. The road was warm under my bare feet as I followed the route William and Jackson had taken up the hill. Houses lined the road and I tried to keep to the shadows, so those on the verandas wouldn't see me. I caught glimpses of large groups of people squeezed around tables, eating, drinking and smoking, but I didn't stop. None of them was William.

As I hiked up the hill, the houses became larger and further apart. A dirt road curved off into the dark, bisected by a deep gouge from what looked like a motorcycle. I smiled and followed the muddy trail.

It led to a house high off the ground, surrounded by a veranda that could only be reached by steep flights of stairs. Two familiar motorcycles were parked at the foot of the stairs closest to the road and masculine laughter drifted down from the house above.

"To not having nagging wives to tell us not to drink too much!" Glass clinked and liquid glugged. "Ah, but I'll miss her 'til she returns from Scotland. So why aren't you married yet, McGregor? Too ugly for the ladies?"

"I couldn't keep them off me in Scotland. It's why I left. Too much choice. There was this one girl on the way here, though..."

"What happened? Did she see your face? Did you belch at dinner? Or did she listen to you for long enough to realise you're naught but a bag of wind?"

"No, none of those things. The ship sank and she was thrown into the water. There were sharks and...the poor girl didn't make it."

"You're not one to let sharks get between you and the woman you love! You're a McGregor, man, one of the descendants of Red McGregor. Why didn't you jump in and save her?"

"I would have. For that girl, I would have,

but I was in another lifeboat. I didn't even know she was in the water until the sharks had taken her from me. Nothing left but a few scraps of bloodied clothing. It was years ago, but she haunts me still."

Jackson laughed loudly. "And I thought you were serious for a minute there! A ghostly, naked, young woman who haunts you. I bet this paragon haunts your best dreams."

"I've had enough to drink for one night and it's time I headed off to bed. Tomorrow we have the biggest locomotive ever built to haul up to the workshop at Drumsite and God knows that'll be hard enough without a hangover. My thanks for the drink and I'll see you in the morning."

"Sweet dreams of sweet girls, McGregor! Tomorrow, you'll remember you work on the devil's truncated tit, mining bird shit to send back to England. Welcome back!"

I waited in the cool night air as the lights in the house were slowly extinguished before I crept up the steps. The house was huge —

much larger than the one I'd shared with Merry D'Angelo in Fremantle. Yet this one seemed just as empty. I padded through spacious living rooms that looked barely lived in, but I assumed that was because of William's absence. That would change once he'd unpacked his things and settled in, I was sure.

The sound of snoring summoned me to the bedroom where he slept. Netting hung from the ceiling, shrouding the bed and the man sprawled face-down across it.

"William," I breathed, not knowing what else to say. The robber crabs had stolen my tongue – so many months of learning to speak his language and I was lost for words now I faced him. "Oh, William." I stared down at his sleeping form, touching my fingers to the netting that separated us.

He shifted in his sleep and the snoring ceased.

"My God, he was telling the truth. You're McGregor's ghost!" Jackson sat up and thrust the netting aside, staring avidly back. "My name is William, lass. You can haunt my bed for as long as you like." He coughed. "At least until my wife returns home."

"I seek William McGregor. He was here. Where is he now?"

"He's in the other house — the new one on the corner by the cliff. Don't keep the man up too late — I need him to help me with the locomotive in the morning." He held out his arms. "Are you sure you won't stay, lass?"

My heart drew me to William, but caution kept me here. "I will sing you to sleep, if you wish," I offered, lifting my voice in song before he had a chance to refuse. I wove a melody of slumber and peace, with an undercurrent of memory loss, for I didn't want him to remember me in the morning. Such was the price of safety.

When Jackson snored one more, I slipped down the steps and into the darkness, following the road to the corner, the cliff…and the man I loved.

William's front steps were gritty with salt

beneath the soles of my bare feet. Movement caught my eye as a robber crab lumbered under the steps, where I could see the lumpy outline of a coconut.

The doors were open to let in the night breeze, much as Jackson's had been, so it was easy to slip between the billowing curtains and into William's house. Without snoring, I was forced to search the rooms, looking for him, but finally I did. He slept in one of the rooms facing the plateau – one of the few without windows overlooking the ocean. Perhaps it held too many bad memories for him – or perhaps this side of the house was more sheltered from the salt spray the swell carried up the cliffs. I noticed William's luggage stacked up against the wall, together with my trunk, sandwiched between two of his. At least I would have clothes to wear this time.

The bed creaked beneath him as William tossed in his sleep. I could see his face, so I knew I'd made no mistake this time. The man before me was William and I needed to tell him so much. But he might reject me or embrace me with open arms. I had no idea how much he'd changed in the time we'd been apart. So, coward that I was, I stood beside the bed, letting my eyes drink their fill of the man I loved.

He was clean-shaven, so the hard lines of his face were in clear view. Even lying in bed, he looked imposing – bigger than most men I'd met. Few were taller than I, but William was both taller and broader. His powerful arms could lift me as easily as I scooped up a snapper – and he had, the night the *Trevessa* sank. When I'd tripped, he'd taken me in his arms and carried me to the lifeboat, entrusting me to the crew before he climbed aboard the lifeboat himself. He'd risked his life to save mine many times over, pulling me from the raft to the *Trevessa* in the first place. If only he'd held tight to me in the lifeboat so I couldn't have left him to seek vengeance and justice and all those things that had seemed important at the time, but didn't matter now.

All that mattered is that we were together now. My heart dared to beat in hope.

"William," I said softly, brushing aside the netting between us so I could touch him. "So long I've waited…"

"YOU!" he shouted, startling me. "Wasn't it enough that you followed me around in Fremantle and on the *Islander*? You have to disturb my sleep here, too? I won't speak to you, I won't acknowledge you, I have nothing left to say to you except GET OUT OF MY HOUSE!"

For the first time, I felt fear as he leaped from the bed and stalked toward me, menace in every movement. "William, please," I began, backing slowly away.

"No William, no please and nothing else. I said get out!" He pointed at the door and I stumbled through it, blinded by tears and tripped by the dying hope that seemed to catch at my ankles.

Tears welled up and overflowed. I had to get out before he saw my weakness. I hurried down the steps and out to the cliff. A wave splashed against it and I tasted salt. Home.

I jumped.

Thirty Eight

I blinked my water eyelids into place and the tears ceased as if they'd never been. Mermaids didn't cry. We fed the undeserving bastards who broke our hearts to the sharks instead. A fate they richly deserved – and one that made me feel so much better than silly tears.

But not tonight. It would take time to assemble a school of sharks and work them into a frenzy, before luring my prey over the cliff into their waiting jaws. William could live another day.

I darted off into the water, looking for a suitable cave to sleep in while I planned his demise. The island's cliffs were peppered with caves, both large and small. Some of them stretched great distances beneath the rock, carrying and bouncing sound from distant points of the island. Idly, I wondered if William's screams as the sharks devoured him would echo through the caves after he died.

A strange line in the stone caught my eye and I swam closer to investigate. It looked like someone had deliberately carved symbols in the rock outside a particularly large cave entrance. Yet the carvings were well below the waterline – far deeper than most humans could swim. My kind, though…in fact, the symbols looked like the ancient ones carved in the reef at home. We'd once had a written language, my teachers had told me, but we'd left it behind with the old city when we migrated to the Indian Ocean. None today could read them, though all the teachers agreed that the most common set of four symbols meant, "Our Indian Ocean home." And the symbols here matched the same pattern, though these were far more ornate than the roughly scratched ones at home. My people had been here before. But how long ago?

Curiosity consumed me, so I entered the cave. The peculiar mixed echoes told me this was one of the far-reaching ones, tunnelling far beneath the island as if some huge, ancient shipworm had drilled out its home here. As I swam through them, I marvelled at the smooth surfaces of the tunnels, undoubtedly sanded by centuries of pounding waves. But not completely smooth. The walls were scratched with shallow marks, cut close together all over the walls, ceiling and floor. A closer look told me it was writing – tiny scratched symbols, like those outside the cave, but thousands of them. All bunched up together like the words in a book.

I followed the engraved tunnel, noticing

side branches but staying with the writing. Who did this? Why had I never heard of it? And was she still here?

If she was, she was very old and I'd invaded her home without permission.

Hesitantly, I started to sing. Very quietly, at first, until the cave chambers picked up my song and reflected it back to me, when it didn't matter how softly I sang – the words carried through every tunnel. I sang of loss, of loneliness and my confusing desire for both ocean and land. But no one answered.

I burst through into air, not realising that I'd been swimming upwards, and into a cave only half-filled with water. The ceiling here was bare of words, for they only stretched up the walls. Yet this chamber was different. A shallow ledge held the rotting remains of a seaweed hammock, still fastened to the wall on one side and trailing through the water like the hair of a corpse. The wall above the bed had ornate letters that I understood:

Dubhan Draak van de Zwartelijn

Beneath it were the deeply carved numbers:

1603

I murmured the unfamiliar words in my head until I realised I did understand them. They just weren't English. Yet the language was immaterial – it was the meaning that shocked me. Dubhan the dragon from the Black line, 1603. That was perilously close to when my people had arrived in this ocean – yet there were no tales of dragons here. The only children's tales that mentioned dragons were warnings about how we shouldn't believe everything we hear, least of all myths, because they had claimed more than one curious mermaid in the past. One lost girl's name stuck in my mind because she bore the same name as my grandmother – Aurelia.

Smaller letters, marked with shallower cuts, spelled out more names. As if the stone had read my mind, there it was:

Aurelia Meermin van de Goudenlijn
Sephira Draaksdochter van de Zwartelijn
1801

Aurelia of the Gold line was my grandmother and Sephira, my mother and her daughter, was born in 1801. If these words were true, then my mother was both more and less than she'd let me believe. Than she'd told the Elder Council.

Draaksdochter. Dragon's Daughter.

I sat down on the ledge, dazed, tracing the words with my fingers. It couldn't be true. Dragons had died out in the wars between our kind and humans, centuries ago. The Black line had been the first to go, for they'd started the war. At least, that's what I'd been taught. How much of it was true? If the Black line had survived in a dragon, this Dubhan, in the Indian Ocean long enough for him to father a child on my grandmother…that meant the blood of the last Black dragon ran through my veins, too. The rage, the desire for power, the drive to fight beyond all reason…came from him.

No wonder Mother kept this a secret. She had more of the madness than I did – her father was a Black dragon. The one who started the war, if the stories were to be believed.

I shifted the trailing kelp from the ledge, lifting the submerged end up to the wall where it had once been pinned. It was too short and narrow for an adult – this tiny hammock wouldn't have fitted anyone bigger than a toddler. This was where my infant mother had slept, as her dragon father carved the walls and kept her mother captive.

I stared at the strange symbols, wishing with all my heart that I could read the words my grandfather had written more than a century ago. One day, I swore, I'd find someone who could teach me.

Thirty Nine

The primal roar of male voices woke me from sleep I hadn't planned. To my disoriented mind, it sounded like they were inside the cave with me, but a quick glance around told me it was the travelling echoes, playing tricks on my ears. Yet it was so loud…

I followed the sound through the only tunnel I could find that led upward. It narrowed quickly, but I could see light up ahead. Direct sunlight lanced through the water before me and I halted in the shadows. If there were angry humans ahead, I didn't want them to see me. Not in my naked human form, nor as I was now – gills, tail, fins and all.

Besides, I'd heard this sort of primitive chanting before and then it had meant one thing – violence.

A loud cheer rang out and then the general buzz of conversation. Silence fell. Flesh smacked against flesh and I heard the crack of bone. A splatter of liquid rained on the soil.

Whoops and cheers erupted over the sounds of more blows, though no more bones breaking.

The chanting resolved into words. "Lee, Lee, Lee…" The sound had a wistful desperation, as if they wanted what Lee might deliver but feared it would never come.

Another blow ended in a crunch, crushing all hope for Lee as the voices chanting his name fell silent. A smaller number of voices took up a different chant. "Tuan, Tuan,

Tuan…"

If there was fighting, William would be here. And if William was his opponent, Lee didn't stand a chance.

A body thudded to the ground. All chanting ceased and was replaced by quiet mutterings in Chinese.

My heart leaped into my throat – who had fallen?

"That's enough for this week, lads. Lee got in a lucky hit. Maybe next time he'll beat me. Worth a month's pay to the winner who does." William's voice calmed my panic. Lee had fallen and he'd survive, too.

I almost screamed in surprise when William's head plunged into the water, not three feet from my hiding place. I choked back the sound, staring at his face to assess his injuries. His nose was bloodied, but that seemed to be all the damage he'd taken. While I sighed out my relief in a stream of bubbles, he withdrew his head, leaving a small cloud of blood twisting in the water as it diluted to invisibility.

"Be careful, Tuan. A dragon lives in the Grotto cave. Maybe he will take vengeance for your victory over one of his people."

Several men laughed, including William.

"Fighting a dragon. Now that sounds like a battle worth singing about. At least for an hour or so, after I've had some whisky. You lads get back up to Settlement or you'll miss dinner."

I waited in my dark tunnel for the sounds above to fade. It took perhaps fifteen minutes before I could no longer hear their voices, and another five before I dared to emerge into the shallow pool. Sunlight turned it a glowing aquamarine, warming the waters so all I wanted to do was stretch out and luxuriate in the unexpected warmth. I sighed blissfully. No wonder Dubhan had chosen this cave for his home – a warm bath at the top, plenty of fish in the ocean that he didn't have to share with anyone and an island to himself, if I'd judged the ages of the island buildings correctly.

Footsteps nearby forced my eyes open. As

William came into view, I dived for my tunnel. I heard his shout behind me, but I only moved faster to get away from him. If he saw me like this, I'd have to kill him. No witness to our existence was permitted to live.

I reached the cave where I'd slept and huddled on the ledge. There must have been sinkholes on the surface that led to my cave, for I heard his voice clearly.

"Wait. Please. I've never seen a dragon before. Damn it. Come out!"

I laughed quietly to myself. If he believed the creature he'd seen was a dragon, all the better for both of us.

Forty

I let rip with the mother of all belches, which echoed around the cave like some sort of roaring beast. I smothered a giggle. Merry would have been shocked.

I probably shouldn't have eaten so much tuna, but the big fish's flesh had been so juicy, and it'd been so long since I'd had fresh fish. I didn't want to waste it, either, though the seabirds made quick work of his carcass.

"That's not a dragon. That's the wind rushing into the caves from the cliffs below!" a male voice scoffed loudly.

I blushed in embarrassment. Even if they hadn't known the noise was me, someone had still heard it. I crept up the tunnel to the surface, hoping to hear better if I could get closer.

"The coolies swore there's a dragon in this cave. I thought they were joking, but I saw it yesterday, Jackson. I swear it. A water dragon with a long, blue-green tail, just like they said. It's real!" William insisted.

My heart sank. He'd seen me clearly enough to describe my tail. I hadn't moved quickly enough yesterday.

Jackson roared with laughter. "Did they tell you what their mythical dragon's called? Apalala. Apparently it was a friend of Buddha's, the deity they worship. They're pulling your leg, man, laughing their heads off at your expense. Tell them to keep their japes for the new administrator. Fresh out of the colonial training course, they're ripe for crazy stories. Not seasoned men like us. From ghosts to dragons – pull yourself together, man!"

I could just see the two men standing on the ledge at the entrance to the Grotto. I lay still in the darkness, hoping they couldn't see me.

Jackson walked away and I heard the chugging sound of a motorcycle engine. The sound puttered away, but William hadn't moved. Instead, he stared into the shallow water as if he could will his mythical dragon into being.

"Right, Apalala, is it?" He dropped to the ground and dangled his legs over the ledge, perhaps a foot above the water. "I know what I saw yesterday and I bet you're laughing your damn head off at me now. The manager's calling me crazy. Are you in it with the coolies, making a damn fool of me?" He threw a stone into the pool, splashing water high enough to hit his shoes. He cursed. "I know I'm a fool. Don't need a dragon to tell me that. Fool to take a job here, a fool to stay and a damn fool for everything in between. Everything was fine until that bloody ship sank. I should have known then this was a mistake and headed home. It probably wouldn't have worked, though. I'll never get her out of my head. Never." He jumped up and stalked out of sight. I heard him kick his Triumph into life and motor away.

I crawled into the pool. The warmth didn't touch me today. I drew my tail up to my chest and cried my heart out. Of course I couldn't feed William to the sharks. I loved him too much.

Forty One

Late that night, under cover of darkness, I swam back to Flying Fish Cove. The ladies in the White House were entertaining as only they could – the sound of their giggles, moans and mock-orgasmic screams drifted into the night. I wondered how many men used their services a night – with only a dozen or so ladies and over a thousand single men on the island, they'd be kept busy.

I gave the brothel a wide berth, sticking to the shadows where their lights didn't penetrate. An owl swooped for bats around one of the lights on their veranda, but I didn't pause to watch. My target was a far bigger bird – and not a bird at all.

The road to Rocky Point was deserted but for some ambling crabs, which suited me just fine. William's house was dark, so there was no one awake to notice me tiptoe up the steps and through a side door. My sure steps took me straight to his bedroom, though his snoring could have guided me there. He hadn't snored this loudly on the ship – he'd barely snored at all, except when he'd had a bit of alcohol.

I scanned the bedroom and found the empty bottle of whisky, half under the bed. I didn't understand how he could drink the harsh, burning liquid, but I'd seen enough of humans to know that some used alcohol to burn away the pain in their lives. My heart ached for the man I'd known – how had life driven him to hurt so much that he needed to dull the pain with whisky? What had happened to him in the intervening years we'd been apart?

I reached out to caress his sleeping face. The stubble on his cheeks rasped under my fingers, reminding me of our first kiss on the *Trevessa*. Kisses. I wanted one from him now.

I leaned over, inhaling as if drawing courage from the very air around me. I parted my lips as I gazed at his…open, unseeing eyes. For a moment, it seemed that his eyes met mine, but he didn't see me. His eyelids drifted shut and he grunted as he rolled over onto his side, away from me.

I bit my lip, forcing myself to back away from the bed. Every fibre in my body wanted to slip between the sheets beside him, but I knew I couldn't. The one time I'd joined him in his bunk on the *Trevessa* was a mistake I wouldn't repeat. Even now I still felt the pain of him pushing me away that morning – and he'd already dismissed me from his home once.

Another step. Another.

I bumped into his nightstand and caught the falling book before it hit the floor. It was my copy of Captain Foster's book about their voyage in the lifeboats after the *Trevessa* sank. The book had been open, face-down on the nightstand as if he'd been reading it as he drank himself into a stupor. Now I knew why.

I'd read the harrowing account once. Never again. It was a miracle they'd survived, but some part of the William I'd known hadn't made it to shore. As I left his house and headed for the ocean, I desperately prayed that I was wrong and the ocean hadn't taken his loving heart.

Forty Two

Once in the water, I let the swell carry me. I needed to feel the power of the ocean caressing me as William might never do again.

"Come play with us, Sirena," a dolphin voice chirped.

I opened my eyes to find a pod of spinner dolphins surrounded me. *"How do you know my name?"*

Laughter bubbled through the pod. *"Sirena*

of the Gold line, daughter of Sephira the Elder. The whole ocean knows your name and your voice. You sing so sweetly you can charm humans into believing you are one of them, letting you live among them. And the Elder Council banished you, but now they desperately want you back to teach them your secrets. Fish with us before you return to land-life."

The rumours were true. Dolphins were worse gossips than humans. Yet they had a light-hearted playfulness that humans and my kind lacked. And I was hungry. *"I will,"* I replied.

There was more playing than fishing in what we did, but I hadn't laughed so hard in a long time. Spinner dolphins are known for their aerobatics and I could leap with the best of them. It did my heart good to enjoy the moment with the marine mammals, though I intended to return to my grandfather's cave before daylight.

When the sun rose, the light caught the yellow fins on the fish I'd caught for breakfast and I dived for the cave entrance, swimming slowly up the carved passages until I surfaced in the cavern that had become my home.

"…don't know why they don't just scrap the hot bowl engine and replace it with something more modern that doesn't break down every other day. Every day, I swear it's only a matter of time before one of the coolies comes down from Ross Hill to tell me I need to fix the water pumps to keep the supply running to South Point…" William's voice said, a little muffled by the vegetation growing around the sinkholes to the surface.

I dropped my fish on the ledge and swam for the pool above.

William's legs dangled off the ledge as they had yesterday, but his voice meandered instead of sounding angry. "That's the funny thing about water supply. You never think about it unless there isn't much of it and you have to work out how to get it. I mean, here we are in the middle of the ocean, surrounded by water, but if the water pump breaks, none of that's any good. We'd have nothing we can drink.

"It was like that in the lifeboat, too. The shipping company put big, tin tanks of water in their lifeboats, with lids that you had to screw off to get into them. But when you put twenty men in a boat, it doesn't go very far. We had fourteen gallons of water on our boat when the *Trevessa* sank — less than a gallon for each man, enough for two days and we were at sea for three weeks.

"The first time it rained, the captain insisted we take down the sail. I thought he was crazy and said so, but he made us hold it out like a cover over the boat to catch water. And when he poured it all into the empty water tank, I realised he knew what he was doing. It was the strangest thing. Sitting in an open boat in the middle of the ocean and a cheer would go up with the first drops of rain. We'd sit there getting soaking wet, licking the water off our faces and squeezing the rain out of our hair into tins so we could drink it. It sounds absolutely foul and it probably tasted it, but to me the brackish water I squeezed out of my beard was ambrosia." He laughed and slapped his thigh.

I settled on the floor of the tunnel, listening avidly to his tale. His animated voice reminded me of the tales he'd told me on the *Trevessa*, which I hadn't understood at the time.

"After that, I helped them hammer funnels out of the empty milk tins — my God, after a week, how we hated condensed milk, but there was nothing else but impossibly hard, dry biscuits to stave off starvation, so we choked it down all the same and tried not to heave it back up again over the side, though many did. The seas were rough the whole way. I think I was one of the only ones who didn't get seasick.

"Anyway, they weren't the sort of funnels you normally use. If dragons use funnels. Do dragons use funnels? What do you use them for? I imagine you probably don't." William laughed again. "Here I am, talking about beards and funnels and you're probably not even listening anymore. Apalala? Is that your name? Are you still there?"

I didn't dare move.

"Apalala. Strange name for a dragon. Is that really your name or just something the coolies made up? The friend of some Eastern god, they say you are, and that the coolies are your people. You're here to protect them or something. This is no place for a dragon now — it's British territory and even this rock is a British colony. The patron saint of England is said to have slayed a dragon, though some say he needed a woman to tame it first. He probably used her for bait to distract the dragon while he ambushed it.

"Beautiful women are always a distraction. Maybe even enough to tempt a dragon. All it takes to distract me today is the memory of a woman. I always was chasing the next adventure, never wanting to be where I was. And now…my next adventure is to sort out the work assignments for the Settlement power station and the two old wood-fired boilers. The Settlement doesn't run without power, and I'll have everyone running to my door come dusk if the lights don't come on. Maybe…maybe I'll come back to talk to you later, dragon, or tomorrow on my run to check the pumps at Waterfall."

William's legs swung out of sight and I heard him fire up the Triumph.

Despite my growling stomach, I didn't move from the tunnel. From Maria the human to Apalala the dragon, I was once more William's silent confidant and the smile it brought to my lips wouldn't leave.

Forty Three

The following day, I listened for the whine of his motorcycle on the road for Waterfall. The moment I heard it, I darted up the tunnel to the pool, eager to see him or at least hear his voice again.

The engine sputtered to a halt in the clearing. His footsteps crunched across the ground and I caught myself wiggling in excitement. I giggled quietly, watching the bubbles float to the surface of the pool.

One foot appeared on the ledge, followed by one leg, then the other.

"Apalala? You here? Did I ever introduce myself before? I'm William McGregor, chief engineer of the guano mine on this godforsaken rock. Excepting yourself, of course. Does being an Eastern deity's friend make you one, too? I don't know much about Eastern religions. The gods all seem to have such peculiar names. Like Apalala. Strange name for a dragon. It puts me in mind of music – with a name like that, I'd imagine you sing. A singing dragon. Do you only sing on land, or do you gurgle tunes in the water, too?"

I snorted with laughter, unable to help myself. A cloud of bubbles rose, bursting just below his feet.

"Captain Foster had this romantic notion that music saved us on that lifeboat. It stopped us from going mad and lifted our spirits. Admittedly, some songs were so stupid you just wanted to strangle the man who came up with the daft tune, but they stuck in your head, all the same. One of the seamen had us craving bacon for three weeks at sea — sometimes with the salt in the air and on my lips, I could almost taste it. We all dreamed about it. Even now the words stick in my head — the daft little tune about bacon."

William cleared his throat a few times before he started to sing:

"I like ham and eggs

I like eggs and bacon

Anybody here says I don't like 'em

He's jolly well mistaken."

He laughed. "There now. It still makes me think of bacon. I'll have to ask my cook to make sure to cook some for breakfast tomorrow, or I'll never get the thought out of my head. There we were on a boat in the middle of the ocean, with naught to eat but biscuits so dry we could barely swallow them, singing about bacon."

He was silent for a few minutes, swinging his legs back and forth. I wanted to reach out to him, to ask him not to go, but as the urge to reveal myself to him increased, so did the nagging voice in the back of my mind that promised one look at me in my true form would be enough for him to run and never come back.

When he spoke again, his voice was subdued. "There…there was another song, too. One I can't listen to now without shuddering. See, Captain Foster knew me well enough from back home. I'm related to his wife, you see. And I…I wasn't doing so well on the lifeboat. Suffered a bit of a shock when the ship sank and I tried to go in after her. He seemed to be able to read my mind and know when I was giving in to despair. And he and the other lads would pipe up with a rousing chorus of this one song. We'd heard it sung in Sydney and Smith had bought a record of it, so we all knew the chorus." William made a sound that sounded like a sob. "Well, by the time we reached Mauritius, every man of us knew the words and some could even sing harmonies to the bloody tune. Sang it that many times, you see. Always the same words, starting with 'There is somebody waiting for me…'" He sniffed and his tone turned angry. "As if she was. It drove me half-mad, knowing the girl I'd saved from a watery grave was snatched from me by the same ocean. The ocean and her sharks took her away from me.

"I'd dream that she was in the water, calling for my help, and I'd reach over the side to pull her up, only to be dragged back into the lifeboat by the other men. I couldn't sleep without seeing her face. One night, when everyone except the men on watch was asleep, I drank the only spirits we had aboard – the stuff in the compass. I was desperate and I hoped even that wee drop could make me forget, even for a moment. But all it did was make me horribly sick. The captain threatened to tie me to the mast like a siren-struck sailor of old if I didn't buck up and show a better example to the other men. And that's when I realised that maybe I wanted to die, but the other men didn't need to see it. We'd already lost two men — two of the firemen, within a day of each other. I'd seen what it did to morale when each of them fell sick and died. Crushed them, it did. But if I leaped over the side in despair, it'd shake them up even more. So I manned up and behaved like I wanted to live. Maybe by the time we got to Rodriguez Island I believed it. I wanted to see if those on the other lifeboat had survived, and I had a job to do here.

"Speaking of jobs, it looks like there's a ship approaching and they'll want every spare pair of hands on the pier to load it up before the swell makes the cove too dangerous. Maybe next time I visit, you'll tell me a bit about yourself, Apalala. What's a water dragon do all day, when you're not listening to me dribble about shipwrecks and sentimental songs?"

He didn't wait for me to reply. He lifted his legs back onto the ledge and walked away. I fled to my cave, so I was already curled up in tears when I heard the sound of his Triumph headed back to Settlement.

I should never have deserted him in the panic the night the *Trevessa* sank. No vengeance was worth this much pain – and William didn't deserve it.

Next time he came to visit me, I swore, I'd show myself to him and offer him the comfort I owed him. It was the least I could do.

Forty Four

My resolve wavered as the day went on, with each scenario I planned. I'd wait until he started talking and I'd swim into the pool in my human form. No, I'd hide in the bushes and slip out when he needed me most. For one heartsick moment, as I tossed and turned and tried unsuccessfully to find sleep, I entertained the notion of swimming into the pool in my true form, then shifting from tail to legs and rising from the water like Venus.

Only if I wanted to kill him to hide the truth before he could return and tell others what I was, I told myself, dismissing the silly fantasy. No man could love a dragon.

I didn't see nor hear William for a few days, though I heard the rattling engine of his motorcycle as he headed down the jungle track to Waterfall and back every morning. Ever curious, on the third, lonely evening, I headed back to Flying Fish Cove to see if I could work out why.

I edged around the ship by the pier. The rock dust billowed off the deck and floated as brown scum on the waves around the ship, marking its partially-loaded cargo clearly. The port workers laboured tirelessly to load the ship, fearful of the swell that could roll into the cove with little warning. Such a swell could smash the ship against the pier and put the whole port out of action for months. Not to mention they wouldn't get paid for the valuable phosphate the ship would spill into the churning waves.

William's house on Rocky Point was ablaze with light. Two dark-haired men sat on the veranda, blowing smoke rings at the fluttering bats. William appeared in the doorway, conversing with another man I recognised as Kaito, the Japanese engineer on the *Trevessa*, who'd given me my first taste of green tea. Before he unwittingly introduced me to jujitsu as he beat William in a fair fight on the aft deck.

The two smoking men rose and all four of them descended from the veranda. A couple clicked on torches while William and the fourth man held some sort of lanterns. William strode ahead, leading them down the track to Waterfall. And the clearing outside the Grotto, where I'd seen William fight before.

My heart leaped into my throat as I dived beneath the surface, undulating out of the cove and around the point before I dared to skim across the waves in the closest thing to a sprint my fins could manage. I needed to reach the

Grotto pool before them so I could see this fight. I couldn't stand the suspense of hearing every blow and not knowing if William was hurt.

I bruised my body against the walls of the narrow tunnel to the surface, but today I didn't care. I needed to find a vantage point where I could see without being seen. I burst through the warm, shallow pool and shimmied up the rope to the mossy rock clearing. The wet season meant there was plenty of jungle around, but it also meant that the broad leaves would block my view. I needed to get somewhere up high.

The cave roof loomed above me and I didn't pause to think of the risks involved in the climb. If I could get on top of it, I could look down on the fighters and hide behind a tree branch if one chanced to look up. I slipped and scraped my shin on the rock, but still I climbed. I could hear voices and there sounded like more than four men on their way here. It sounded like half the miners were tramping the track to the Grotto to watch the fight.

I managed to reach a spot where rainwater had pooled, carving a depression in the rock over the centuries until it was a bowl big enough to hold and conceal a worried, young mermaid. Or me, at least. Unfortunately, it also held a thriving community of curious red crabs. They shied away when I first appeared in their midst, but my stillness seemed to entice them back again. I wanted to sing to them to send them scuttling away, for all sea creatures obey a siren's song, but the approaching men were too close. I couldn't risk them hearing me. For if I could climb this rock, so could they.

It was one thing to reveal myself to William, but to fifty or a hundred men who saved up a week's pay for five minutes with one of the ladies of the White House? It would be worse than my last night on the *Trevessa*, when I'd unwittingly charmed the whole crew with a song.

I crouched lower, hoping the leaves hid me as I peered between them at the shadowy figures marching into the clearing. A few held lanterns or torches, but the dim light made them seem more ghostly than real. They spread out, forming a ragged circle around the edges of the clearing. In the centre, I saw rocks had been laid out in a rough fighting ring. The lanterns were placed at intervals between the rocks, illuminating the stage for the violence that would come. No one seemed to be bothered about the crabs sidling across their ring – they all seemed engaged in a heated discussion. I caught the phrase the Chinese grocer had called the Japanese sailors in the port – *Riben guizi* – and the name McGregor a lot, but my Chinese was too poor to understand much more than that. When scraps of paper started changing hands, I guessed that they were betting on the outcome of the fight.

The crowd parted to allow two Japanese men, followed by William and Kaito, into the ring. The two I didn't know moved to opposite sides of the circle. William set his lantern down on a flat rock.

Both men took off their shirts and passed them into the crowd. One of the miners hung the white cotton on two adjacent rock pinnacles, where they fluttered like ghosts.

William squared up, his hands open instead of clenched into fists. Kaito spread his arms wide, palms up, in some sort of invitation.

"Ready for your rematch, Kaito-san? It was a lucky kick that won it for you last time. Luck favours me this week. I bet even the local dragon will be watching this fight."

Some of the miners laughed and translated the comment to those around them. White teeth caught the light as many more smiled.

"Dragons don't favour *gaijin*. They are tricky, cunning creatures who might make it seem so. I am ready, MacuGuregoru-san," Kaito replied calmly.

I wasn't. But no one cared what I thought.

Kaito aimed the first blow and William's arm blocked it. A jab, a block, a kick, a dodge, another kick, a caught foot, more jabs, a foot released, circling, circling…the two men moved faster than I could fathom, reacting to the other's slightest movement. This dance was far more deadly than the one I'd witnessed on the *Trevessa*. William ducked and wove as sinuously as I could – and that was saying something. The smaller man seemed to have increased his skills, too, for some of his blows landed – though so did William's. Neither stopped to nurse their injuries, though, which I assumed must be minor.

Circling, circling…Kaito thrust his hand up at William's chin and he jerked back to avoid it. Kaito followed up with a kick to William's midsection that folded him in two, making him expel all his air in a shout as he flew several feet to the edge of the ring.

I crammed my fist in my mouth to stop myself from screaming. I couldn't watch this man hurt William. I had to intervene, to stop him, to…

"You have improved, MacuGuregoru-san,"

Kaito said. "Now, you dance as skilfully as the girl fighter on the ship."

The girl who beat him in a fair fight. I jumped to my feet, determined to leap into the ring and end this.

Kaito's eyes met mine and he froze.

William rolled to his feet. "A girl who beat you, Kaito-san. Maybe her ghost whispers instructions to me as we fight, so that I may be just as victorious." He crashed into Kaito, sending him to the ground. I couldn't see what he did to him, but I heard the Japanese man grunt in pain.

I dropped to my knees again, hiding behind the branches that had hidden me so well before.

"MacuGuregoru-san, the winner!" one of the Japanese non-combatants declared. A loud cheer went up from many throats — but not all, I noticed as several miners threw their bets to the ground in disgust.

William offered his arm to Kaito to help the man up. Both bowed to each other, though

Kaito bent lower than William did.

The smack of flesh on flesh became jovial as the miners congratulated Tuan, as they called William, before collecting their lanterns and moving off toward home.

Soon only the three Japanese men and William remained. The two whose names I didn't know made as if to wait, but Kaito waved them on, so they left, too.

"Is it true?" Kaito asked.

"Is what true?"

"The girl who died with the *Trevessa*. Does her ghost truly visit you?" Kaito persisted.

William sighed. "Yes. Every day."

Kaito smiled. "Perhaps she comes to watch you fight. Her spirit will rejoice in your victory today."

"No." William sank to the ground. "I fight to forget. When I'm in the ring, exchanging blows and focussed only on the bout, that's the only time she's not there. It's the only time I don't feel a coward for deserting her."

"I felt her presence here tonight,

MacuGuregoru-san. If she has watched you for so long, then she knows you are no coward. It took four men to hold you back in the lifeboat, but if they hadn't, you still could not have saved her. You must pick your fights, my friend. No man is a match for sharks." Kaito held out his arm and William took it, rising as he grimaced.

"I almost wasn't a match for you tonight. Maybe I'm getting old." William limped toward his lantern and hooked his fingers around the handle.

"Luck smiles on you tonight, then, along with spirits and maybe even a dragon." Kaito inclined his head in my direction and headed off with William trailing after him.

Forty Five

I waited for William to return to the cave, determined to show myself. Kaito had seen me; surely he'd tell William and then William would come looking for me.

When the motorcycle chugged over the rise, headed down to Waterfall, I dived into the bushes and hid, but he didn't stop. I waited for perhaps ten minutes before a robber crab started prodding my foot to work out if it was edible. I rose and stamped my foot to drive it away. The sun shone in the clearing and I'd had enough of hiding. I stepped out into the sunlight, spied a mossy place to sit and placed my behind on it. Pulling my hair down over my breasts, I hugged my knees to my chest, trying to calm my racing heart.

The motorcycle was returning. He was coming to me.

The motor didn't change pitch, like I knew it should. He just kept going to Settlement, without coming to see me. I sagged with a mixture of relief and disappointment. If he didn't know I was here, he couldn't reject me again – I still had hope. But I hadn't seen him.

Every morning I waited and every morning he avoided me. Until one morning, when there was no sun in the clearing. The clouds had been massing on the horizon for days and the increasing swell told me we were in for a powerful storm, much like the one brewing inside of me. All that pent-up frustration and fury and desire and terror and love…I stared at my mossy rock and refused to wait today. The only thing that could calm me was a force more powerful than anything inside me. I needed to swim in the storm.

I slid down the ledge and into the shallow water. I stretched, keeping my heels together, and concentrated on my form. The skin over my legs stretched and fused from my thighs down to my toes, where my flukes extended in a delicate blue fan. I let the colour creep up my body until I could feel the coolness of the change at the back of my neck. I took a deep breath, rolled over and dived.

I knew the tunnels well, so I took them at speed, from the surface all the way down to the end of Dubhan's carved markers at the underwater entrance. I opened my gills to the swell and took my first big gulp of life-giving seawater. A powerful eddy tried to slam me against the cliff face, but I darted away, laughing, revelling in the sensation of the storm swell against my sea-skin. Mine. All this was mine — it was part of the ocean's gift, which no mere human could share. To swim with me now in the maelstrom would cost William his life.

I laughed for joy as the ocean overpowered me and took me in her arms, wherever she wished to go. All day I swam and into the night.

Yet all good things come to an end and so did my energy. When the next day dawned, I rode the waves back to the island and crept up to Dubhan's cave so I could sleep away my exhaustion.

Forty Six

My whole body felt both stimulated and sore, as if I'd had energetic sex all night, but I knew I hadn't. I could only think of one remedy for it – another day of more swimming. I stretched and sighed.

"Apalala? Please…please come out. I've brought my curse with me to the island and I don't know what to do anymore. I thought I could hide from it here, but everything's falling apart here now, too. Everything I touch is cursed."

I leaped up at the sound of William's voice, motivated by many things, including the faint possibility of sex instead of a swim.

"The *Islander* stood offshore for two days until we finally managed to bring it close enough to Waterfall to lighter things ashore. She's just left – even I had to man a boat and I'm the worst sailor we have. The cove is impossible – I've never seen a swell so big. Must be thirty feet or more. Monstrous. It carried away the loading pier and smashed it to kindling on the beach by the coolie houses. And then the waves started eating away at the Settlement road itself – there are waves washing right up to the doors. When the pier went, the waves battered the timbers into the buildings along the shore. The only storm I've ever seen like this was the one that took the *Trevessa*. It's my curse. It must be."

His feet weren't dangling over the pool today. Instead, he paced up and down the ledge as he spoke.

"I thought it would be enough. The pier, all the damage…the swell's starting to go down this morning, so we thought it was all over and safe to move people back into their houses. And that's when the damn plateau came tumbling down. A bloody landslide…boulders as big as bungalows, bouncing down the hundred-foot cliff onto the houses below. Mud moving like a waterfall, all the way to meet the sea in the cove. It's a miracle no one's dead. Instead, now we have a hundred homeless coolies and nowhere to put them but our houses or the Club and Jackson swears it's all my fault – as an engineer, I should warn him when things are going to go wrong and he's right. The ocean's trying to attack us from all sides and the cliffs are fighting back! This place is cursed and it's all because of me.

"I saved that girl from the ocean with my own hands. Pulled her barely alive from that flimsy raft and carried her aboard the ship. I gave her my clothes. I helped her dress. I fed her, protected her, took care of her and I swore to her I always would. Then that storm came and sank the ship. I let her get dragged into a different lifeboat that overturned in the waves and I let her get left behind. I loved her and when she needed me most, I deserted her and left her to die.

"And her ghost followed me here. I can't eat or sleep without seeing her. And I know I'm not crazy because Kaito saw her, too! Here! I wish I'd had a water dragon with me when you might have been able to save her and help me fight off the sharks. So, tell me, Apalala: have you seen my Maria?"

Forty Seven

I slipped into the darkness, out of sight, so I could shift to my human form. My skin paled to cream as my legs parted. I took one more deep breath, blowing water out my gills before I closed them. Kicking hard, I burst to the surface, but William was no longer in sight. I'd been so slow changing that I'd missed my chance.

Perhaps he was headed back to Settlement. I

leaped as high as I could, hoping to catch a glimpse of his retreating back. I saw a flash of white between the trees and I knew it was him. "William, WAIT!" I shouted, scrambling up the slippery rocks. I slipped and banged my knee on the way down, scraping my shin against the rough stone. "Please, William. Wait for me." Slowly and more carefully, I tried to climb up again. Angry tears splashed on my hands, but I persevered.

"I said stop haunting me!" William pounded into the clearing, as furious as I'd ever seen him. "If I could have saved you, I would have. I'd have married you, Maria, I swear it. I didn't want you to die and haunting me won't help. I wanted you to stay in the lifeboat with me! If it helps lay your ghost to rest, then I'm sorry I didn't save you from the sharks. I'm sorry for everything I ever did to you!"

"Marry me? You never asked me to do that, William." I dragged myself over the rock lip and rolled so that I was face-up on the grass, panting. After a moment, I gritted my teeth and climbed stiffly to my feet. As William's words started to sink in, I began to laugh. "I'm no ghost, William. Ghosts aren't clumsy enough to slip while climbing out of this damned pool. Ghosts don't bark their shins and bleed, either. And crabs don't try to nip off ghosts' toes. Get off me!" This last was directed at a curious red crab as I aimed a kick at the creature. It backed away slowly until it decided to return to investigate. The creature's claw prodded my foot, then closed around my big toe. I stomped my other foot to frighten it. "I said – "

A large hand grabbed the crab from behind and lifted it away from me. William's other hand curled around my ankle. "You're not. You're real. My God…" His fingers trailed upward, tickling my thigh and continuing over my hip to my ribs. "Real. You're…" He seized my shoulders and kissed me fiercely. At first, I stiffened in shock at the unfamiliarity of being touched, but I forgot all of that in the blaze of my desire. My uncertainty burned away as I knew all I wanted right now was his body against mine, with nothing between us. My fingers made swift work of his shirt buttons as his tongue danced with mine so expertly it was as if we'd never parted.

He shrugged out of his shirt and coat, one arm at a time, as the other arm held me tightly to him. He threw the clothes over a tree branch, not turning to notice if it had caught them or if the crabs had carried them off. I unbuckled his belt and felt his pants slide satisfyingly down his legs. An awkward moment ensued while he kicked off his boots, socks and pants, all the while kissing me as if he thought I'd disappear the moment he stopped. With nothing but his cotton drawers between us, I knew he wanted me as much as I wanted him.

His eyes followed mine down to his straining shorts and he tried to cover himself with his hand. "I'm sorry. You have this terrible effect on me…"

My hands shook with excitement as I reached for the waistband of his drawers. How many years had I ached for him? Too many. "I know the cure." Creamy cotton flew off into the jungle and I threw myself at him. We both smacked into the mud, my body partially on top of his. I squirmed until I felt him hot and hard against my belly. I sat up, letting my thighs slide open over his hips until my knees landed in the mud.

William caressed my hip with one hand as his other adjusted himself, teasing me with the tip. "Are you sure?"

"No," I admitted. "I might not cure you." I tilted my pelvis and ground my hips against his, enveloping him before he realised what I was doing. His groan made me grin. "I might make you desire me over and over and over again." I anticipated his thrust, riding him hard so he drove deep inside me. It was my turn to moan with pleasure as he matched my rhythm with unerring skill.

"What...then?" he asked breathlessly, pumping harder.

This was better than the first time. Better than

any time. I couldn't think. I couldn't focus on anything but the heat building, pushing, tantalising…

I cried out as he drove me over the cliff of an orgasm. William's tongue caressed my nipple, but with the way my breasts were heaving as I tried to catch my breath, he soon sucked it into his mouth. I dragged air into my lungs and he sucked harder, pulling on my nipple even as my breast lifted with breath. The sound that came out of my mouth was halfway between a moan and a sob, as I squeezed my eyes shut to focus on the exquisite sensation. That wasn't all I squeezed, either as William's answering groan told me he enjoyed the clenching of my thigh muscles and all those between them.

"Maria, you're going to make me…make me…" He slowed his thrusts, pushing deep and then almost pulling out of me, brushing against some nerve between my legs that ignited a little more with every stroke. His eyes stared deep into mine as if he knew exactly what he was doing. "I've dreamed about this.

Dreamed of hearing you shout my name…"

"William, I think I'm going to…ex…exp…William! Oh, William!" The pleasure nerve he was teasing blazed into blinding light and my words were lost as I screamed until I ran out of air and then screamed again. I was dimly aware of William pulling out of me, leaving me with an aching emptiness inside and the ghost of his heat.

"No. I want…more. Please, William, don't stop now," I begged, not caring that I sounded weaker than ever before.

He laughed gently and touched his lips to mine. "I have to, lass. You milked me for all I had. If you give me an hour or two, I might manage another time, but that was…powerful, that was. You've convinced me you're no ghost, but I'm hard pressed to understand how you came to be here. If you insist on more, maybe you can tell me your story in the time it takes me to recover. I wouldn't want to disappoint you, lass."

Disappoint? He was everything I'd

remembered and so much more. I ducked my head to hide my blush and realised we were both filthy from our roll in the mud. "Would you like to come for a swim in the Grotto with me?"

William grinned. "Are you sure you're brave enough for that? There's a dragon that lives in this grotto. I've heard him roaring many a time. Even seen him once or twice. He might mistake a beautiful woman like you for a sacrifice sent to appease him, and take you deep into his lair where he'll hold you captive in the dark…"

I laughed. "Did you never think that I might be your dragon? Come ashore in the shape of a woman to tempt you and lure a handsome man into my lair so that I might have my way with you forever?"

William's laughter joined mine. "You tell a good story, Maria. Almost as good as mine. You're forgetting the day we met when I found you floating, barely alive, on a flimsy raft. You're a woman and a tempting one, too, but not a dragon."

I hid my smile as I followed him into the water. William didn't believe in mythical creatures — not even after making love to one.

Forty Eight

William washed quickly and sat on my rock to dry in the sun, but I floated in the aquamarine water, hoping it could cool my ardour long enough to let me tell William my story – or as much as I was willing to tell.

"Just watching you in the water takes me back to the night the *Trevessa* sank. I saw blood in the water…sharks…your clothes, shredded and bloodstained, floating in the waves…it took four men to hold me back, or I'd have dived in the water after you. If I'd known you were still alive, nothing would have stopped me. Not four men or forty. Your ghost has haunted my dreams and my waking moments every day since then. How did you survive the sharks? How did you make your way here? How did you find me? How did you learn to speak?"

I laughed and waved my hands to stem the tide of his endless questions. "I'll tell you and answer as best I can, but I must start with that night. Sciarra dragged me to one of the little lifeboats and he launched it. He stood over me with a knife and threatened me if I didn't do what he wanted."

"He was a complete savage," William snarled. "I should have beaten his head to a pulp instead of just knocking him out. Or thrown him overboard for the sharks. Hanging's too good for men like him…"

"The ocean meted out her own justice to him that night. The waves tipped our boat so that the only person Sciarra's knife cut was himself before we were both thrown in the water. He was bleeding and the sharks honed in on him. While I clung to our overturned boat, he died screaming." I couldn't hide my smile.

William's eyes looked huge, they were open so wide. "How did you survive? Why didn't they eat you?"

For a moment, I considered telling him the truth. That I could control sharks and no shark in the sea was stupid enough to attempt taking a bite out of me. No. William could never know what I was. Not now, not ever. Even if he did believe me, which he never would.

I took a deep breath. "The waves righted the lifeboat, but she was full of water. I hauled myself over the side and started bailing the water out. First with my hands and then I found a tin of some horrible, sweet milk. I drank the milk and used the tin to empty the boat. Scooping up seawater and throwing it over the side. Over and over again until my arms ached, but I kept going, even as the waves sent more water in. And when I couldn't lift my arms any more, I found a sail in one of the lockers. I wrapped myself up in it and fell asleep across one of the benches.

"I woke up alone in the lifeboat, but more water had crept in overnight. I drank my milk breakfast and had two tins to bail with, so it went faster, but I soon tired myself out. I didn't have the strength to assemble the mast and hoist the sail, so I promised myself I'd do it the following day. I curled up under the sail and slept.

"When next I woke, it was dark and my boat had stopped moving, but I heard voices. My lifeboat had been picked up by the *Trevean*, come to rescue survivors from the *Trevessa*. They'd thought the lifeboat was empty, but when one of them looked under the sail, they found me. I was bruised and battered from…from everything that happened on the *Trevessa*, and I had no pants, so they thought the worst. I was given into the care of a female passenger – a widow by the name of Merry D'Angelo. A teacher. She found me some clothes and helped me learn to speak your language while the *Trevean* searched for you and the others in the *Trevessa* lifeboats. For three weeks, we steamed up and down the ocean, looking for some sign of you, but we found nothing.

"They gave up the search and headed for Fremantle, their destination port in Western Australia. Merry let me stay with her until I found a job – until she found me a job – and then I stayed on as a paying lodger. I think she was lonely. She did so much for me – so much more than I deserved. All while I earned the money to start searching for you and pay my passage to wherever I needed to go to find you." I was so carried away with my story that I didn't stop when I should have. I fought to hide my blush. My cards were on the table and it was too late to hide them now.

William seized on my words. "You had to work? Maria, tell me you didn't…that you didn't sell your body for me?" The desperation and guilt in his eyes made my heart ache.

I burst out laughing. "You think I…that I…I'd let a man touch me for money?" I fought to control myself. As if I'd let just any man touch me and live, when even those I loved dared death for the privilege. "I worked in a fish market. I sold fish. Occasionally, I helped with sorting the catch. And sometimes, when they were a man down, I got to go out on the boat and taste the salt spray as we sliced through the swell of the open ocean." I couldn't keep the desire from my tone. I knew now that I would always lust for the power of the ocean. I could never surrender to a simple life on land.

Colour crept back into his relieved expression. "I can't imagine you as a fishwife. Didn't it smell terrible, working with fish every day?"

I stared at him. Salt, seaweed and fish were the smell of home. How could they ever be anything else to me? "I guess it's just something I became used to," I ventured cautiously. My foot bumped into the rock and I pushed back, propelling myself into the middle of the pool. My own reflected wave bounced off the rock and swept over my torso, chilling my breasts before they met warm air once more.

William climbed back into the water, his eyes on me. "I've never seen a woman bathe naked before and I must say it's the most arousing thing I've ever seen." He swallowed noisily. "Maria, if you still want to, I'm ready for you."

I looked down to discover he certainly was. I pushed my body effortlessly through the water until his body slid between my parted legs. I wrapped my legs around his waist as he grabbed me, both of us panting to connect in the most primal way possible.

"Oh, yes," I moaned as William thrust deep inside me before his passionate kiss stole my willing tongue.

Forty Nine

I let the sun dry me as I watched William dress himself. A robber crab had made off with his drawers, but a quick search revealed both the thief and its haul and William had already pulled his pants on over his underthings.

"Why aren't you getting dressed? Where are your clothes?"

I lost all composure in helpless laughter. "I felt I didn't need them," I answered. Clothes only got in the way while swimming. "William, it will take too long to explain why, but I don't have any with me."

William stared for a second, then turned his head away. He shrugged out of his jacket and held it out to me with shaking hands. "Please take it. I can't take you home like this. I'll go to the Settlement and bring you back something to wear. You can't wander around here naked – the mosquitoes will eat you alive and if one of the other men sees you…"

I might have to kill him.

I took the jacket. The smooth leather was warm in my fingers, much like his skin had been when we'd made love. Both his eyes and his tone had chilled now as if the sinking sun had stolen all his warmth. "William. Is it so hard to look at my body? You called me beautiful once. Has my appearance changed so much?"

"No," he said hoarsely, his gaze flicking across my body. "You look exactly the same as you did then. But looking at you now makes me want to…do all sorts of things to you." He swallowed. "Things we shouldn't do until we're married. I'm sorry, Maria, but I can't seem to resist you. I take one look at you and I forget that there's anyone else in the world but us. But if I take you home like this…people will ask questions. They'll ask where you came from and why you aren't properly dressed. They'll think and say things about you that aren't true. I want you to come with me and be my wife, Maria – I've wanted it since I met you on the *Trevessa*, and you've haunted me every day since I lost you, because no other woman compared to you."

I stepped closer. "If you still want me, then my heart is yours."

William grabbed my hands, though I still held his jacket in one. "Of course I still want you. I've never stopped wanting you and even now I don't want to let you go. Maria, I offer you my heart, mind and body, and everything I own, to take care of you and protect you for the rest of my life."

I swallowed. His heart. He gave me his, but he already had mine. "I…William, you already have my heart. I…" He kissed me into silence.

"I'll speak to Jackson and see if you can stay with him and his wife until the *Islander* returns and we can go to Singapore to get married. Damn, Jackson won't have room for you – his house is full of coolies whose houses were buried in the landslide. Maybe one of the other married men can take you in – or if Jackson sends them to the Club instead, where they should have gone in the first place, then he and Anne will take you. Damn fool thinks he can keep the Club for the white folk when it's the best place to billet people when things like this happen. I wish you could stay with me, but you can't until we're married or people will talk."

I stiffened. "I will not live in a house with strangers again without you, William. We've been parted for long enough. People always talk. I say let them."

He shook his head. "They'll say bad things

about you and I'll defend you, just like on the ship, but I won't be able to silence everyone, Maria. They'll call you…they'll say that you're no better than the ladies in the White House."

My eyes blazed. Of course I was better in bed than those poor, tired women, endlessly servicing men they didn't love. "Then introduce me as your wife and say I arrived on the *Islander*. Tell them that we are already married instead of the truth."

His eyes lit with hope. "You'd do that? Pretend to be my wife until you are? We'll take the next ship to Singapore and make it official." He paused as if the idea had dealt him a stunning physical blow. "You'll be my wife. I'll make you the happiest woman alive, lass. I swear it." He kissed me fiercely, holding me so tight that his shell buttons dug into my breasts. He seemed to realise it as he let me go. "But I can't take you back to Settlement like this, even if it will be dark when we get there. Put the jacket on."

I slipped my arms into his leather jacket.

The sleeves hung down past my hands, but the waistband sat snugly above my hips. I started to button it up, but my breasts were too big for the top buttons. The jacket squashed them together like an old-fashioned corset, pushing them up instead of covering them.

"Oh, you can't wear that, lass. Maybe…maybe my shirt?"

I removed the jacket with considerable relief and let him strip his shirt off and put it on me. For a moment, I was reminded of the first time he'd helped me dress on the *Trevessa*. The touch of his hands still quickened my heart, just as they had then.

"It's hard to believe this isn't a dream, Maria," William said slowly as he buttoned his shirt over my breasts. A deep kiss followed which neither of us seemed to want to end. "I need to get you home. Do you think you can sit on the motorcycle behind me if I ride really slowly?"

My heart leaped at the thought of my first motorcycle ride with William. I looked at the

Triumph, then recoiled in horror as I realised the only place to sit behind him was a small, wire shelf on top of the rear mudguard. For the first time in my life, I longed for underwear. "I'd rather swim back to Flying Fish Cove," I replied without thinking.

William burst out laughing. "But it's miles! You can't do that. Honestly, a motorcycle's nothing to be afraid of. You just hold on tight and I'll keep you safe. I promise."

Was he not seeing the same motorcycle I was? I strode over to the Triumph and tapped the hefty shock-absorbing spring beneath the rider's seat. "Would you want this thing between your legs? What if you stop suddenly?"

He turned redder than the crabs milling around our feet. "I never thought…"

I winked. "Put a proper seat on the back of that and give me a pair of pants, and you can take me for a ride anywhere you like."

After some consideration, I agreed to sit in the seat while William wheeled the Triumph back to Settlement. Of course, this meant he had his arm around me all the way back, which suited us both just fine.

Fifty

The sun had well and truly set by the time we reached Rocky Point and William's house. The house was a blaze of light and a pith-helmeted figure paced the length of the veranda.

William helped me off the bike and kept an arm around me as I walked stiffly toward the steps. At the top, he recognised the pacing man. "Jackson?"

"Where on Earth have you been? And who

in blazes is she?"

William stepped in front of me, as if to preserve my modesty. "May I introduce my wife, Maria?"

Jackson spluttered but didn't manage to say anything intelligible.

I slipped around William and held out my hand. "Mr Jackson. The moment the lighter from the *Islander* landed, William insisted on taking me up to see a dragon in a grotto. We found no dragon, but I wanted a dip in the grotto." His eyes were transfixed by my bare legs. I hurried to find some excuse for my state of undress. "Some of the local crab inhabitants stole my things while we were –" I coughed delicately "– swimming." I blushed.

To my relief, there was no light of recognition in Jackson's eyes. He took my hand and kissed the back of it. "A pleasure, Mrs McGregor. No wonder your husband kept you a secret."

"Maria, you should go and change for dinner," William said quickly, taking my arm.

"I'll show you where your things are." He hustled me into the house, guiding me to his bedroom before he shut the door behind him. "Now what? I don't have any women's clothing and if I ask any of the servants, it'll be all over the island by dawn." Inspiration lit his eyes. "No, that's not true. Some woman's trunk was mixed up with my things in Fremantle and it ended up on the *Islander*. So when we landed, someone brought it up here the rest of my luggage. It's all yours, Maria, if anything fits you." He dropped to his knees and flipped open the rusty catch. William lifted the lid and gestured proudly at the contents.

I laughed softly and knelt beside him. I rummaged through my things for a suitable dress and appropriate undergarments to go underneath it. I threw them on the bed and sighed at the creases in my dress. "Everything has been in here too long – they need to be aired and ironed." I pulled his shirt over my head and dropped it beside my clothes. I dressed quickly, buttoning the front of my dress over the brassiere before I turned to face William. "Is this…will this be all right?" I glanced down at my bare feet. "I have shoes, too, and I still need to comb my hair…"

William's arms closed around me, pulling my body against his. "I've never seen you look so beautiful. This is the first time I've ever seen you in a dress."

My startled eyes lifted to meet his. Surely he'd seen me wear dresses in Fremantle – I'd been wearing my best on the day of the motorcycle race. "Don't be silly. Of course you have. At the race at Ascot, in Armstrong's motorcycle shop, on the boardwalk outside the South Beach Hydrodome. You barely glanced at me, but I know you saw me."

His hands gripped my shoulders. "That was really you? I thought your ghost was haunting me again. Everywhere I went, it seemed like I saw you! And the way you stared at me, as if you blamed me for leaving you in the water like the coward I was. If I'd known you were alive, nothing would have kept me from you, I swear."

Finally, I understood. "That's why you wouldn't look at me or even speak to me? You thought I was a ghost – that I wasn't real." It was my turn to apologise. "I thought you were deliberately ignoring me and being incredibly rude. When I boarded the *Islander*, all I wanted to do was kick you." I hesitated, then continued, "That's why I stole your chocolate cake."

"My cake?" His expression turned blank before realisation dropped his jaw. "You mean the one that went missing on the voyage here. You stowed away on the *Islander*?" At my nod, he ploughed on. "That night on the foredeck. You watched the dolphins beside me, didn't you? You were so close. All I'd had to do was reach out and I could have held you in my arms again."

I smiled wistfully. "You still can. I'm here now."

"And the trunk…that trunk is yours, isn't it?"

"Of course. One of the lumpers carried it to the *Islander*'s hold for me, which was a godsend, as I didn't think I could have dragged it another step, having lugged it all the way from home to the wharf. I think I would have cried if I had to drag it up from the cove to this house, too."

"All this time, you've been here – hiding in the jungle!" He shook his head in disbelief. "I should stop staring at you and dress for dinner."

While he changed his clothes, I dug through the trunk for my comb, the precious tortoiseshell one William had given me on the *Trevessa*. My hair had dried in salty tangles on the long walk home and I sat on the edge of the bed to sort them out.

I'd barely made any headway before I felt William sit on the bed. He threw one leg on the blanket beside me, pressing closer so I could feel the heat of him at my back. His fingers closed around mine and the comb. "Let me take care of that for you." Willingly, I surrendered the comb and my tangled tresses to William.

His skilful hands rapidly tamed my hair, then bound it into a braid, just as he had on the *Trevessa*. This time, I thanked him with a kiss.

William took my hands and pulled me to my feet. "Shall we?" He offered his arm and I took it.

Fifty One

When we entered the dining room, Jackson rose from his chair. I glanced at William, who didn't seem to find this unusual. William helped me into my seat, before taking the one beside me.

"My house is full of coolies whose houses were buried in this morning's landslide. A man can't think with so much noise in the house. We'll have to find somewhere else for them to stay until the houses are rebuilt or dug out," Jackson said. "You have plenty of space here. You could take a few. Take the pressure off my wife and me."

William poured himself a glass of water and gulped half of it down before he remembered me. He poured me a drink, too, which I sipped carefully.

"Why didn't you just move them in today while I was working? Seems that would have been easier for everybody," William said.

Jackson laughed – nervously, I thought. "I don't know what you've done, but all the coolies are terrified of you. Wouldn't set foot in your house without your permission, no matter what I said."

William gave a tiny smile, which he hid behind his glass as he took another drink.

Just like on the ship, it must have been the fighting bouts. William had built up some sort of respect through them. Whether it was his ability to beat any of them in a fair fight or the offer of prize money if they won, they wouldn't act against him.

"Mrs McGregor," Jackson began. "Surely you can find it in your heart to help the poor unfortunates who have no homes. There was a landslide this morning in the cove and many of the mine workers' homes are buried beneath tons of mud. They need a place to stay and you have so much space in your home."

"This is my first night in a new house in a new place, Mr Jackson," I replied carefully. "I'm not sure I'm ready to accept strangers in my house, too. I did see a big, new building down near the port, though – some sort of club, William told me. That looks like a good place to house people temporarily." I saw William hide his approving smile.

Two Chinese women entered the room carrying steaming bowls, which they set down before us. I picked up my spoon and tasted the soup. From the grease it left on my lips to its general lack of taste, it left me with no desire for any more of the stuff.

Jackson tried again. "McGregor, explain to

your wife how we do things here. Christmas Island is no place to be delicate. Why, you already have strangers – servants – in your house!"

"But they sleep in the servants' quarters or at home with their own families," I said. "Not in the house. Mr Jackson…"

He slammed a hand down on the table. "Now, see here, woman. I'm the island manager here and what I say goes!" He rose. "I'll send them over in about an hour. Have your servants prepare rooms for them." He didn't move as if he was waiting for some sort of surrender from me – or for William to rein me in.

William slurped his soup as Jackson looked from him to me.

"Well?"

William set down his spoon. "You're the island manager, but it seems to me that my wife is mistress of this house. Now, I haven't seen her in a long time and I've missed her a great deal. I wouldn't want to be on her bad side this evening." He winked at Jackson.

Jackson turned an interesting shade of red. "I'm sure this crisis takes precedence over how much you've missed your wife, however much you might love her. I'm heading home now and when I get back, you'd better be ready for…"

I rose, noting that I matched Jackson in height. "Mr Jackson, if you return in an hour, I think you'll find that there are no servants to answer the door because I'll have sent them home. Neither William nor I will answer you, for we'll be in no state for company. And if you decide to billet some poor people on us tonight, I assure you they'll get no sleep, for William and I have a lot to catch up on and William has promised me a delightful night which will not be a quiet one." I met his eyes and didn't drop my gaze.

"I'm sure I don't know what you mean," Jackson said coldly. His blush said otherwise.

I grinned. "Then you should probably discuss that with your wife. I hope she can enlighten you on what you're doing wrong. Good night, Mr Jackson."

William laughed. "Good night, Jackson. I'll see you in the morning and if I'm not too tired, I'll see if I can help you find somewhere the coolies can sleep until they finish rebuilding."

The angry island manager stormed out.

A bat flew through the open door and landed in my luke-warm soup, splattering the stuff everywhere. I burst out laughing. This island had the strangest, most intrusive wildlife I'd ever encountered.

The two women returned to clean up the mess. A few minutes saw the soup bowls gone and our main course set on a clean table.

William lifted his wineglass to toast me. "To my beautiful wife-to-be, small victories and the sanctity of our home."

I lifted my glass in response and we both drank.

William swallowed quickly and added, "All this talk of a delightful night has inflamed my imagination. I'm afraid if you say much more,

I'll lay you on the table beside the plates and devour you instead."

I laughed and blushed. William seemed to be reading my mind.

Fifty Two

I kept my word to Jackson – within an hour, we were done with dinner and William's staff had shuffled down the steps to their own homes for the night. Anticipating a night in bed with William, I eagerly led the way to his bedroom, unbuttoning my dress on the way. I threw it over a chair and struggled with the fastenings of my brassiere. I'd been swimming naked for so long that I'd forgotten about the tricky things and no matter how much I craned my neck, I couldn't see to unfasten the damned thing. It felt like I'd managed to moor it to my own hair.

I glanced at William, but he had his back to me as he unbuttoned his own shirt. "William, can you please help me with this?"

Reluctantly, he dragged himself across the room and fumbled around against my back. I chanced a look over my shoulder at him and saw the man had his eyes closed. I burst out laughing and his eyes popped open. "What?" he asked grumpily, yanking my braid free from the hooks.

I let the brassiere slip to the floor and turned around. "You still won't look at me, William." I slid my bloomers off and kicked them away. "Am I so horrible?" I cupped my breasts and lifted them like a corset might. "It's these, isn't it? They remind you of melons, too."

"Oh God…sweet and round and ripe and…why did you have to say melons? I won't be able to sleep for thinking about them now. As if lying beside you weren't enough to keep me awake. I'll be a gentleman, I swear – I won't lift the hem of your nightdress, though it'll kill me not to." William covered his face with his hands.

I took his hands in mine. "What nightdress? Do you think I'd wear something so silly on our first night together? I'm not sure if it's the same among your people, but among mine a couple's first night together is an occasion for pleasurable intimacy." Carefully, I covered my breasts with his hands.

William tore his hands away. "When we're married, yes, but not before. I will worship your body from dusk 'til dawn on our wedding night, but tonight….tonight…"

"Things are much simpler among my people than yours. What you call a marriage is an agreement between two people, made before witnesses, yes? Among my people, that is all it is. Two people agree to be partners in life and they inform someone in authority. It's the pledge that makes the partnership, not how loudly it's proclaimed." I shrugged. I'd seen the elaborate weddings in St Patrick's Basilica in Fremantle and I couldn't imagine ever wanting such ceremony for anything in my life. "I don't understand. Once the partnership is official, the night of celebration begins. We…we said our pledges in the clearing by the Grotto and told your angry superior, Jackson, that I am your wife. Now you tell me our words are worthless and you won't touch me while we share a bed? That I must wait and undertake another dangerous sea voyage with you – one that might separate both of us forever?" I gestured at my body. "Don't you want me?"

He swallowed. "More than anything." He stared at my breasts as he seemed to struggle with something in his head. "I can't bear to lose you again, lass. I want you to be mine in every way possible – yesterday if I could make it so. You are…by your rules, we are already…married?" I nodded slowly. "Which means that you want…nay, expect me to make love to you tonight?"

I managed an uncertain, watery smile. "Please?"

His eyes held mine and I didn't dare look away. I stared into the ocean depths through his irises and I knew I was home. And in the darkness of the depths, a light kindled. His lips landed on mine and sucked away my breath like a drowning man might. Powerful arms lifted me off my feet, holding me tight against his hard chest as he carried me to the bed. He laid me down reverently, the feather pillows crackling under my head. His eyes never left mine as he stripped off the remainder of his clothes and sat on the edge of the bed.

Strong hands cupped my breasts as if they were as fragile as glass. "These," he began, "are sweeter and softer than any melon." He trailed kisses up from my belly to my breasts, then pressed his lips to each nipple in turn. His tongue traced a spiral around my right nipple, then my left. "I've never seen anything more beautiful, nor tasted anything so delicious." His fingers caressed my breasts. "And here…right here, beats your warm heart, alive and promised to me." A fervent kiss landed on my left breast.

I stroked his hair. "Yes." It came out as a whisper.

He leaned over further so that his muscled chest lay against my breasts, and he kissed me deeply. His tongue overpowered mine, reminding me of the storm currents that had stroked my body in the cyclone, caressing me with raw power that left me breathless.

We broke for air and I found myself panting. He truly had stolen my breath, but I'd have given it gladly.

He stroked my thighs and I willingly parted them, my desire rising as he knelt between my legs. He bent to kiss my breasts again, brushing his lips down my belly to my navel. His hot breath tickled my skin. "I'm going to claim your body, lass, claim it so completely that nothing will ever part us again." He didn't wait for me to reply. He thrust his tongue inside me, licking my lower lips so hard that I shuddered in pleasure. "As wet and salty as the sea I plucked you from. I'm damn glad I did." His fingers held me open as his tongue plundered my insides until a wave of pleasure engulfed me.

"William…William!" I gasped, hearing him chuckle as he carefully kissed my thigh.

"I'll never tire of hearing you say my name like that, lass, but you're a hard woman to resist. Are you ready for more?"

I looked deep into his eyes as I reached for him. "Oh, yes."

I cried out for joy as he surged into me more powerfully than the swell into the caves below, sending wave after wave of ecstasy through my body until his shout echoed mine. This wasn't the ocean's triumph at all. This was mine and William's alone.

ABOUT THE AUTHOR

Demelza Carlton has always loved the ocean, but on her first snorkelling trip she found she was afraid of fish.

She has since swum with sea lions, sharks and sea cucumbers and stood on spray drenched cliffs over a seething sea as a seven-metre cyclonic swell surged in, shattering a shipwreck below.

Demelza now lives in Perth, Western Australia, the shark attack capital of the world.

The *Ocean's Gift* series was her first foray into fiction, followed by her suspense thriller *Nightmares* trilogy. She swears the *Mel Goes to Hell* series ambushed her on a crowded train and wouldn't leave her alone.

Want to know more? You can follow Demelza on Facebook, Twitter, YouTube or her website, Demelza Carlton's Place at:

www.demelzacarlton.com

Books by Demelza Carlton

Siren of Secrets series
Ocean's Secret (#1)
Ocean's Gift (#2)
Ocean's Infiltrator (#3)

Siren of War series
Ocean's Justice (#1)
Ocean's Widow (#2)
Ocean's Bride (#3)
Ocean's Rise (#4)
Ocean's War (#5)
How To Catch Crabs

Nightmares Trilogy
Nightmares of Caitlin Lockyer (#1)
Necessary Evil of Nathan Miller (#2)
Afterlife of Alana Miller (#3)

Mel Goes to Hell series
The Devil's Work (#1)
See You in Hell (#2)
Mel Goes to Hell (#3)
To Hell and Back (#4)
The Holiday From Hell (#5)
All Hell Breaks Loose (#6)
The Devil Goes to Heaven (#7)

Romance Island Resort series

Maid for the Rock Star (#1)

The Rock Star's Email Order Bride (#2)

The Rock Star's Virginity (#3)

The Rock Star and the Billionaire (#4)

The Rock Star Wants A Wife (#5)

The Rock Star's Wedding (#6)

Maid for the South Pole (#7)

Jailbird Bride (#8)

Romance a Medieval Fairytale series

Enchant: Beauty and the Beast Retold

Dance: Cinderella Retold

Fly: Goose Girl Retold

Revel: Twelve Dancing Princesses Retold

Silence: Little Mermaid Retold

Awaken: Sleeping Beauty Retold

Embellish: Brave Little Tailor Retold

Appease: Princess and the Pea Retold

Blow: Three Little Pigs Retold

Return: Hansel and Gretel Retold

Wish: Aladdin Retold

Melt: Snow Queen Retold

Spin: Rumpelstiltskin Retold

Kiss: Frog Prince Retold

Reflect: Snow White Retold

Roar: Goldilocks Retold

Cobble: Elves and the Shoemaker Retold